Smitten with Strudel

Smitten with Strudel

A Smitten with Travel
Romantic Comedy

ELLEN JACOBSON

Smitten with Strudel
Copyright © 2021 by Ellen Jacobson

Print ISBN: 978-1-951495-21-3
Digital ISBN: 978-1-951495-20-6
Large Print ISBN: 978-1-951495-22-0

Editor: By the Book Editing

First Printing: February 2022

Published by: Ellen Jacobson
www.ellenjacobsonauthor.com

For everyone who has always dreamed about being a super secret spy. Someone has to stop the bad guys and save the world—why shouldn't that person be you?

CONTENTS

CHAPTER 1
THE PROBLEM WITH
MARSHMALLOWS

There are three things I can't stand more than anything in the world—marshmallows, nylons, and secretive men.

I'll apologize in advance if you're one of those people whose eyes light up at the thought of s'mores or rice krispie treats, or if you have a drawer full of hosiery. But I think we can all agree that guys who are closed books, who never tell you the whole truth, those are the worst.

Given my recent run of bad luck, I'm not surprised that I'm having to deal with two of my pet peeves on the first day at my new job, namely marshmallows and nylons. Fortunately, since I've sworn off guys, cryptic, cagey men won't be a problem I have to deal with. Right?

Please tell me I'm right.

I really need to be right about this. I'm nervous enough starting this new job. The last thing I need is another guy barging his way into my life and turning everything upside down.

Take deep breaths, Isabelle. In, out. In, out.

I repeat this mantra to myself for a few moments. After my last exhale, I feel better. It's okay to feel anxious, I tell myself. It's okay to have these feelings.

Then I remind myself what a great opportunity this job is. An American girl like me working on a European riverboat cruise line. What's not to love? Sailing to exciting ports of call. Exploring quaint towns and bustling cities. Learning about new cultures. Meeting interesting people. Eating delicious food. Who wouldn't be thrilled?

I straighten my shoulders and look around the reception area of the *Abenteuer*, the riverboat that will be my home for the next four months. We're currently docked in Mainz, a German city on the Rhine River. The boat has just undergone some renovations, and everything sparkles and gleams. Unfortunately, the maintenance crew is still working on the air-conditioning system—a necessity for these warm summer days—so I'm dripping with sweat, which isn't a good look when you're hoping to impress your new manager and colleagues.

After wiping my brow, my eyes light on Sophia Papadapolous, the bubbly Greek front desk receptionist assigned to conduct my new employee orientation.

She's still brandishing a tray of marshmallows. "Isabelle, are you sure you won't try one? It's a new recipe that the executive chef created. They're amazing."

Did I mention the marshmallows are green? Not an attractive shade of green either. More like something you'd see in a petri dish in a lab experiment.

I shake my head. "No, really. I'm not hungry. I just —"

I can't finish my sentence because Sophia has shoved a marshmallow into my mouth.

Did I mention that they're enormous? Seriously, who needs marshmallows this big?

I try desperately not to gag, but it's hard not to. I feel like I'm choking on a sugary ball of cotton. I try to swallow it, but the spongy texture freaks me out. I can't do it. I really can't.

I frantically try to find a tissue in my purse to spit it out into, but all I come up with is a crumpled up twenty Euro bill. If I spit the marshmallow into it, I doubt that anyone's going to accept it as legal tender after that. Would you take money covered in marshmallow? No, of course you wouldn't.

While I'm pondering my options, Sophia prattles on about the executive chef's other dessert creations.

There's no box of tissues in sight. I have no idea where the restrooms are, and I'm starting to freak out.

Someone clears their throat behind me. I turn and see a man wearing a gray suit. He's not wearing a tie, and his black shirt is unbuttoned at the collar. I catch a glimpse of gold chain before my gaze drifts upward past a jawline with the perfect amount of stubble to a pair of icy-blue eyes framed by hair so blond it looks like a whiteout in a snowstorm. Normally, I'm attracted to men with dark hair and eyes, but there's something about this guy that's making me rethink that.

Not that I'm thinking about this stranger in that way. Definitely not. Sure, he's handsome, but I can tell from the look on his face that he knows women fall for him left and right. And that smugness . . . that's definitely not my type.

His eyes sweep over me before focusing on Sophia. "Excuse me, miss. Is this where I check in?" he asks with a crisp German accent.

"You must be Erich Zimmerman. We were told you would be boarding the boat a day early." Sophia presents the tray to him and smiles brightly. "Marshmallow?"

"No," he growls.

Sophia's hands tremble slightly when she sets the tray down. As she prints out his registration form, Erich gazes at me intently. Pointing at the left side of my face, he says, "Your cheek is swollen."

Why yes, it is swollen. Swollen because there's a giant inedible marshmallow pressing my cheek out like I'm some sort of hamster.

Of course, I'm thinking this, not saying it out loud. I was raised not to talk with my mouth full, thank you very much.

Erich cocks his head to one side, waiting for a response. When I don't reply, he turns his attention back to Sophia.

I gently stroke my cheek. Is it possible this marshmallow is burrowing through my tooth enamel? Are cavities already forming? Is a huge dental bill looming in my future? What's the world record for keeping a marshmallow in your mouth without swallowing it?

As these questions swirl around in my head, I spot a crisp white handkerchief tucked in the pocket of Erich's suit jacket. He must have seen me staring at it, because he hands it to me. I immediately spit the disgusting, gooey marshmallow into it.

Then I do the unthinkable—I hand the handkerchief back to Erich.

Why? I don't know. Maybe because my mom always told me to return things promptly after borrowing them?

Erich eyes the sticky handkerchief in his hand, then thrusts it back at me. "Keep it."

As he asks Sophia where he can wash his hands, I

feel my face grow warm. I'm mortified. Beyond mortified. Within seconds of meeting this suave debonair European guy, I've embarrassed myself beyond belief. I'm sure my face is almost as red as my legs.

Oh, yeah, I forgot to tell you why I hate nylons so much. Every time I wear them, my legs break out into a rash. And when I'm nervous, like I am now, my rash breaks out with its own rash.

I haven't worn nylons since my days in the Air Force. Back then, nylons were required when wearing a skirt. That's why I usually opted to wear pants with my dress blues. But here on the *Abenteuer*, pants are not an option with my uniform. The HR department was very clear—no skirt, no nylons, no job.

In hindsight, I should have opted for "no job." I should have stayed back home in Texas. I should have kept my dead-end job working at the mini-mart. I should have . . .

Enough with the "should-haves," Isabelle. Deep breath. In, out. In, out.

My breath hitches in my chest when I realize Erich is looking me up and down. Why is he so handsome? No one should be this good-looking. Especially not a guy whose handkerchief I just spit a marshmallow into.

Erich's eyes widen ever so slightly when his gaze reaches my legs. I'm pretty sure it's not because they're long and shapely. No, if I had to hazard a guess, he's horrified by the red, blotchy hives covering them.

"You really should get that looked at, Isabelle," he says. "You wouldn't want it to interfere with your morning run."

He nods briskly at Sophia and me, then turns toward the restroom. As he walks away, I crumple his handkerchief in my hands and try to resist the urge to scratch my legs.

Then I do a double-take. How does he know my name? I'm not wearing a name tag, and I'm positive he didn't overhear Sophia say my name. I'm certain that we've never met before. I furrow my brow as another thought sinks in—and exactly how does he know I go running every morning?

* * *

While I'm pondering how Erich Zimmermann knows who I am, a beefy hand clamps down on my shoulder.

"I should have you fired for what you just did," a gravely voice hisses in my ear. "Spitting into the handkerchief of a VIP guest—that is *verboten*."

I spin around and find a stocky woman in her early sixties glaring at me. Her beady eyes narrow as she cracks her knuckles, one by one. My stomach twists into knots and I feel the hives on my legs multiplying. This woman is seriously scary, like a villain out of a James Bond movie.

Sophia nudges me and whispers, "You should apologize to Frau Albrecht. Otherwise . . ." Her voice trails off, leaving me to fill in the blanks as to what fate awaits me if I don't immediately express my contrition.

I startle, recognizing the woman's name from the paperwork the cruise line sent me. Frau Albrecht is the Director of Guest Services. In other words, my new manager.

"Um, I'm sorry, ma'am," I splutter. "It's just that marshmallows—"

She holds one of her beefy hands up, cutting me off. Her knuckles look swollen. I'm guessing she won't be able to get her gold signet ring off easily.

"Do not make excuses," she says slowly, emphasizing each word.

Frau Albrecht's German accent sounds harsh, unlike Erich's, which sounded smoky and sexy. His voice was the kind that makes you feel all tingly from your toes all the way up to your—

Whoa, Isabelle. Stop thinking about that man's accent. You swore off men, remember?

As usual, my inner voice is way more rational than the rest of me. I shove all thoughts of Erich out of my mind.

"You're not going to fire her?" Sophia asks Frau Albrecht.

My new manager purses her lips. "Unfortunately, Head Office won't let me."

The way she says "Head Office" makes it sound like the ultimate authority, one that cannot be defied.

Sophia furrows her brow. "But I thought you made all the hiring decisions on board the boat."

"Normally I do," Frau Albrecht says. "But for some reason, Head Office is earmarking Isabelle Martinez for special treatment. They think she is an exceptional hire. Goodness knows why. She's never worked aboard a cruise ship of any kind, and her only customer service experience comes from working at a mini-mart." She spits out "mini-mart," like it has left a foul taste in her mouth.

Sophia turns to me. "A mini-mart? You mean like one of those stores at a gas station?"

"It wasn't located at a gas station. It was next to a dry cleaners," I say, as if that makes my former dead-end job so much classier.

"Huh." Sophia cocks her head to one side. I can't tell if she's trying to figure out what "dry cleaners" means in Greek or if she's trying to find something polite to say about mini-marts.

"Ah, Herr Zimmermann." Frau Albrecht oozes charm as she gives the VIP guest a wave.

Chewing on my bottom lip, I watch Erich walk toward us from the restroom. His hands look marshmallow-free. I can't say the same about mine. Awkwardly clutching his handkerchief in my fist, I look down at the floor.

Frau Albrecht starts to speak in German to Erich,

but he interrupts. "English, please."

"My deepest apologies for your treatment earlier by a member of my staff." I can feel Frau Albrecht's beady eyes boring into me. She grabs the handkerchief from me, probably instantly regretting that choice given how sticky it is, then says to Erich, "We will have this dry cleaned for you immediately."

"That's unnecessary," he says. "Isabelle can keep it. For allergy sufferers, a handkerchief can come in handy."

My eyes widen. I take a step toward Erich. "How do you know I have allergies? What are you, some kind of stalker?"

"Isabelle, don't be rude," Frau Albrecht says sharply. "Herr Zimmermann is a personal friend of the owner of the cruise line and our VIP guest. You must treat him with respect."

"It's fine. Isabelle and I are just bantering," Erich says in a soothing tone. Then he turns to me, "Isn't that right?"

"Uh, yes," I say hastily. "Bantering. That's what it is."

No, that's not what it is. This is not bantering. This is just plain weirdness. What kind of stranger drops in facts that he shouldn't know about you into casual conversation? I need to get to the bottom of this.

Erich bows slightly. "Now, if you'll excuse me, ladies, I will get settled in my stateroom."

As he walks up the staircase that leads from the

reception area to the deck above, Sophia whispers to me, "I'm glad you're not getting fired. I have a feeling things are going to be interesting with you on board."

Frau Albrecht clears her throat, then gingerly hands me back the handkerchief. "I believe this is yours. Now, about your duties."

As she explains what's expected of me as a desk receptionist, I notice that Erich's handkerchief is monogrammed. Except the initials aren't "EZ" for Erich Zimmermann. Instead they're "STW." Why is he carrying someone else's handkerchief?

Frau Albrecht's cell phone rings, mercifully stopping her lengthy description of the proper use of a three-hole punch. Apparently, the secret is in how you apply pressure. While she listens to the person on the other end of the line, she hands me a stapler and motions for me to practice using it. This office equipment tutorial is almost making me miss my days working at the mini-mart.

Sophia and I exchange glances when Frau Albrecht screeches into the phone, "What? Head Office wants me to do what?"

She listens for a few more moments—enough time to crack her knuckles several times over—before hanging up. Turning to me, she says through gritted teeth, "You're no longer a desk receptionist."

Sophia squeezes my hand. "You're firing Isabelle? I thought you couldn't do that?"

"No, I'm not firing her. I'm . . ." Frau Albrecht

pauses to take a deep breath, grimaces at me, then continues. "I'm promoting her."

"Promoting me?" I ask. "Promoting me to what?"

"Congratulations," Frau Albrecht says flatly. "You're our new tour manager."

"Tour manager?" Sophia abruptly releases my hand. "But she can't be. That's Maria's job."

"Head Office has transferred Maria to another role. She'll be based in London."

"No, that's not possible," Sophia says. "Maria is my best friend. She would have told me if she was being transferred."

"It was very sudden," Frau Albrecht says.

Sophia pulls her phone out of her pocket, but before she can dial her friend, Frau Albrecht stops her. "You won't be able to reach her. Her flight has already taken off."

"Fine. I'll speak with her later," Sophia says. "But why Isabelle? If anyone should be promoted, it should be me. I've been working on this boat for three years, and Maria was training me to take over her role one day."

"Yes, you would be much better suited to the role." Frau Albrecht turns and glowers at me. "But Head Office instructed me to give the job to Isabelle."

I hold my hands up. "I don't want it. Give it to Sophia. Besides, I don't even know what a Tour Manager does."

Frau Albrecht ignores me and goes into the small

office behind the front desk. She returns a moment later and thrusts a large binder in my hands. "Everything you need to know is in here. We have passengers boarding tomorrow for a weeklong Rhine River cruise. I hope you're a quick study."

Before I can ask any other questions, Frau Albrecht tells Sophia to join her in the office. I stare at the binder and gulp. I'd give anything to be back at the mini-mart right now.

I'm about to push open the office door and insist that Frau Albrecht give Sophia the job when I overhear the two of them talking.

"But that job should have been mine," Sophia says.

"Don't worry," Frau Albrecht says. "She will fail. I guarantee that by this time tomorrow complaints will be so numerous that Head Office will have no choice but to fire her and give you the job."

"Are you sure?"

"Absolutely," Frau Albrecht says. "She is completely unsuited for the position. One way or another, I'm going to make sure she leaves here in disgrace."

I straighten my shoulders and hug the binder to my chest. Challenge accepted, lady. The only one who's going to be disgraced is you.

Then reality sinks in and I slump against the wall. How in the world am I going to pull this off?

* * *

The clock is ticking. I have less than twenty-four hours before the passengers begin boarding the *Abenteuer*. They'll be expecting their tour manager to greet them, answer any questions they may have about the cruise, and brief them about the itinerary and ports of calls. And they'll expect that their tour manager is knowledgeable about the history and culture of the areas they'll be visiting.

Boy, are they in for a surprise.

As of right now, all I know about the cruise is that we start in Mainz. From here, we'll sail north, first stopping at Rudesheim, Koblenz, and Cologne in Germany, then onward to Amsterdam in the Netherlands, where the trip will end and the passengers will disembark.

And that's pretty much the extent of what I know. Detailed knowledge of each port? History and culture of the region? What time dinner is served? I don't have a clue.

I shift the binder in my arms. Time to get cracking. I've got a lot to learn.

The reception area is bustling with activity as crew members get the boat ready for departure, so I decide to head to the library, where I can hopefully get some peace and quiet.

I race up the stairs, then through the opulent lounge, where passengers can gather for drinks, play card games, or just sit quietly and look out the windows, taking in the sights. The entrance to the library is next to the sleek wooden bar.

Pushing open the door, I breathe a sigh of relief. The small room is deserted. I kick off my heels, and my feet sink into the plush carpet. I set the binder on a coffee table, then inspect my legs. The itchiness is unbearable, but I remind myself for the millionth time not to scratch them.

It's not easy. What's the point of having an itch that you can't scratch? There are some mysteries about the design of the human body that I'll never understand—Why in the world do our ears keep growing? What's up with having an appendix since it serves no purpose? Itchy skin is right up there.

I plop onto the couch and stare at the binder. I know my therapist and I have talked about the importance of embracing change, but this is ridiculous.

I should quit. There's no shame in quitting, right?

Okay, there's a little shame, but I can live with shame. It wouldn't be the first time. But there's the little matter of my bank account balance. Usually, I'm very careful with my finances. But I've spent more than I planned on this European adventure. Now all I have left is that crumpled up twenty Euro note in my purse. Since I won't get my first paycheck until next month, I was counting on free room and board to get by.

I look down at the amethyst ring on my right hand, and my eyes tear up. Memories of my grandmother's funeral flood back. "She wanted you to have this," my mom had said to me. "She was a strong woman, just like you are." That was right before I joined the Air Force. I thought I was a strong woman at the time. But so much has happened since then. Nowadays, I'm scared of my own shadow and panic when there's any change to my routine.

After wiping my eyes, I grab my phone and send a text to my mom. It's time to swallow my pride and ask for help. I know she'll be happy to loan me some money, but I hate being in this position.

While I wait for her to respond, I absent-mindedly scratch my legs. When I realize that I've drawn blood, I shake my head. Why am I still wearing these ridiculous nylons? If I'm quitting this job, it's time to take these babies off.

I walk out of the library and head to the restrooms at the far end of the lounge. Of course they're closed for cleaning. Just my luck. I could go to the restrooms on the deck below, but I don't want to run into Frau Albrecht until I'm sure my mom can help me out financially.

The itching is insane. I rush back to the library. There's no one inside, so I close the door and hitch up my skirt. I strip the nylons off one leg, then as I'm tugging the other side over my other ankle, I hear a familiar German voice ask, "Do you need assistance?"

Startled, I try to pull the nylons back on and straighten my skirt. Things don't go as planned, and I end up on the ground with my nylons twisted in a ball in my hands and my skirt turned around so that the zipper is in front. It's a good look . . . not.

I squeeze my eyes shut. If I can't see who's talking to me, they can't see me, right?

"May I assist you?" the man asks again.

Hoping it's not who I think it is, I crack open one eye. Then I groan. It's him. Or at least it's his shoes. Why I recognize Erich Zimmermann's shoes, I have no idea. It's not like I'm into men's shoes. Now men's suits, those I notice. Especially ones that emphasize their broad shoulders. Like the gray suit Erich had on earlier.

I crack open my other eye. Is he still wearing that suit?

Stop thinking about what Erich's wearing, Isabelle. You're lying on the floor clutching a pair of nylons in your hands. Is now the time to be thinking about menswear?

I squeeze my eyes shut again. Maybe he'll take the hint and go away.

"Here, let me help you up," Erich says, oblivious to my hint.

Taking a deep breath, I open my eyes and see his outstretched hand. I extend mine, but he frowns.

Of course. That's the hand with the nylons in it. He probably thinks I'm trying to give them to him, like I tried to give him back his marshmallow-encrusted handkerchief. He's smart, I'll give him that. Too smart to accept anything I try to hand to him.

I extend my other arm, and he pulls me to my feet.

"Thanks," I mutter.

"Your leg is bleeding," he says matter-of-factly.

I gasp when I see the bloodstain on the carpet. Why couldn't I have resisted the urge to scratch my legs?

As I try to blot it out with my nylons, Erich walks over to a small buffet table by the window and pours a glass of water.

Really? Is he going to watch me try to clean this up while having a refreshing drink?

"Try this instead," he says, pulling a fresh handkerchief out of his pocket and dipping it in the water. After he hands it to me, he leans back against the wall.

Okay, he was helpful with the wet handkerchief, but it's really annoying how he's calmly standing there watching me.

I finally manage to get the blood out, then Erich helps me to my feet again.

Glancing at the handkerchief in my hand, I say, "I don't suppose you want this one back either."

He shakes his head. "No, you can keep that one as well. Although, it isn't as fascinating as the first one I gave you."

Since when did handkerchiefs become fascinating? "Okay, thanks. It'll make uh, an interesting souvenir."

"Souvenir of what?"

I shrug. "My short-lived tour manager job."

Erich furrows his brow. "Short-lived?"

"Yeah, I'm going to quit. I'm not cut out for this."

"Quit? No, you're not quitting," he says firmly.

"Uh, yes, I am." I shove the handkerchief in one of my jacket pockets and the nylons in the other. "Not that it's any of your business."

"Oh, but it is my business." Erich's eyes grow steely. "There's no way you're quitting. Not after all the trouble I went to arranging for you to get this job."

I arch an eyebrow. "You got me this job? I don't think so. I never even met you until today, mister."

Erich folds his arms across his chest. "We may not have met before, but I can assure you that the reason you have this job is because of me. It's the perfect cover for our mission."

I arch an eyebrow. "Our mission?"

"Yes, we've been tasked with stopping an international arms deal."

CHAPTER 2
THE THIRD STREET THUGS

I double over with laughter, not caring that I'm making snorting sounds. Stopping an international arms deal? Is this guy for real?

As I wipe tears away from my eyes, Erich asks coolly, "Do you think letting terrorists get a hold of weapons is a laughing matter?"

The expression on his face is so serious that it sends me into another round of uncontrollable laughter. When I finally catch my breath, I ask, "Did my friend Mia set this up? I've warned her about her practical jokes."

Erich frowns. "You can't tell Mia about this. You can't tell anyone. This is top secret."

"Top secret, of course." I try not to smile as I pretend to be zipping my lips.

"You're not what I expected," Erich says after a beat.

"We just met. How could you have expected anything?" Then my eyes widen and I start to edge toward the door. "Hey, wait a minute. You knew what my name was, that I'm a runner, and that I suffer from allergies. Have you been following me?"

Erich holds up his hands. "No, I haven't been following you. It was in your file."

I stop in my tracks. "My file? What file?"

Erich looks at me as though I'm stupid. "Your Air Force file."

"How did you get a hold of my file? You realize it's a serious crime to hack into a government database."

"Of course, I didn't hack into anything." Erich shrugs. "Not that I couldn't have if I wanted to. Piece of cake."

Wow, not only is he an oddball, but he also has a huge ego. This situation is getting stranger by the moment. There's no way some random German dude could have gotten a hold of my file. To be honest, I don't know whether to flee or stay and find out how he knows so much personal information about me. And this thing about terrorists? Someone has seen too many spy movies. He probably likes to look at himself in the mirror and say, "Bond, James Bond," out loud while pretending to fire a gun.

The obvious conclusion is that he's some sort of stalker. Time to make my exit. I edge toward the door.

Erich lets out an exasperated sigh. "Isabelle, what is wrong with you? Stop playing around. We have serious work to do. The organization is counting on you. I need to begin your briefing."

The way Erich emphasizes "the organization" and the tone of his voice makes my body tense. And his use of the term "briefing"—I haven't heard that since I was in the Air Force.

"Wait a minute, is this . . ." My voice trails off as I realize there's more going on here than I initially thought. This isn't a practical joke, and this mysterious stranger is no stalker.

Erich grabs my arm and pulls me toward him. Then he whispers in my ear, "Does 'the third street thugs' ring a bell?"

The minute Erich utters that code phrase, I know for certain that this is real. When I left the Air Force, my commanding officer told me that if anyone ever approached me saying, "the third street thugs," it would be a sign that they needed to reactivate me for duty.

My breathing becomes shallow and my pulse races. Feeling faint, I press my hands against Erich's chest to steady myself. "The initials on your handkerchief—STW," I say faintly. "It was a signal."

"That's right, Isabelle," he says. "A signal that the organization needs you. You know what STW stands for—save the world—and we need your help to do it."

"So what you said about stopping an international

arms deal is real?"

Erich tips my face up so that I'm staring into his icy-blue eyes. "Yes. I need you. We need you."

"Why me?" I cringe as I hear my voice squeak.

"Because of your particular talents."

"Talents? Me?" Could my voice get any squeakier?

Erich lowers his face so that his lips are brushing against my earlobe, sending tingles down my spine. "Well, you were the Youth Scrabble Champion when you were fifteen and you took third place in the National Scrabble Tournament in your freshman year of college. Undaunted, you came back the following year and took the championship," he says softly.

I can't help myself. I start laughing again. This time it's a slightly maniacal laugh. I step backwards and press my hands to my mouth. Taking a few deep breaths, I shake my head. "Scrabble is going to stop an international arms deal? What's next? Bringing down the Mafia with Candyland?"

A slight smile plays on Erich's lips. "Ah, Candyland, the kids game. I'll suggest that to my superiors."

"And who exactly are your superiors?"

Before Erich can answer, I hear Frau Albrecht's voice over the loudspeaker. "Isabelle Martinez, report to the dining room. I repeat, Isabelle Martinez, report to the dining room."

Erich points to the doorway. "You better get going. Frau Albrecht doesn't seem like a woman you want to keep waiting."

I wring my hands together. "But Scrabble, an international arms deal . . ."

"I'll explain over dinner. Meet me at eight in the reception area. I know a place in Mainz that makes great pfälzer saumagen. You'll love it." Erich gives me a warning look. "Be on time. I don't like to be kept waiting either."

Can you believe it? After Erich dropped that huge bombshell, my stomach grumbles at the sound of Pfälzer Saumagen. I have no idea what it is, but considering I missed lunch, and breakfast was ages ago, anything sounds good.

"Hungry?" Erich asks.

"Famished." My phone buzzes. "That's my mom. I texted her about quitting."

"Text her back and tell her it was a mistake. We need you in this tour manager role." He holds up his hand, forestalling my questions. "Like I said, I'll explain over dinner tonight."

"Fine," I mutter as I type a response. When I look back up, Erich has vanished.

Frau Albrecht's voice booms over the loudspeaker again. "Isabelle Martinez, report to the dining room immediately."

I slip my shoes back on and grab the binder from the coffee table. I guess there's no harm in playing along for now. Time to report for duty. But you better believe I'm going to get some answers from Erich before I decide whether to stick with this "Scrabble-playing tour manager save the world from terrorists" gig.

* * *

When I reach the entrance to the dining room, I see Frau Albrecht standing in front of the double doors, tapping her foot while she stares pointedly at her watch.

"You're late," she barks.

"Sorry. I was . . ." I shift uneasily as I try to figure out what to say.

"You were what?"

Realizing that I can't exactly explain to her that I've spent the past thirty minutes with her VIP guest talking about a top-secret mission, I tap my binder. "I was studying."

"Good," she says. "Then you know how long the Rhine River is."

"Uh, not exactly."

"It's 1,230 kilometers long. That's 765 miles for you Americans. These are the types of facts that you need to have at your fingertips," she huffs.

I sigh. I'm not sure what's going to be harder—pulling off the tour manager role or stopping an international arms deal.

"Now, hurry along," Frau Albrecht says. "Sophia needs to finish your new employee orientation. It's important that you're familiar with how the meal procedures work."

When I walk into the dining room, I spot Sophia putting a chef's hat on her head.

"How do I look?" she says playfully to a man wearing kitchen whites.

He rubs his bare head, then reaches for his hat. Sophia tries to dart away, but he grabs her by her waist and tickles her. She finally yields and gives his hat back to him.

As he places it back on his head, he says, "You look better without a hat."

Sophia tucks some stray hair back into her bun and grins at him.

Then he motions at her uniform, adding, "You'd look even better without that on too."

Okay, I really don't want to see how far they take this, so I clear my throat.

Sophia frowns when she sees me. "Oh, you're here."

I smile and restate the obvious. "Yep, I'm here."

Extending my hand, I start to introduce myself to Sophia's companion, but she interrupts. "Isabelle is the girl I was telling you about who spit out your marshmallow."

The man purses his lips. "You spit out Auguste Renoir's marshmallow? Auguste Renoir will not forget this."

"Who's Auguste Renoir?" I ask.

Sophia strokes the man's arm. "*This* is Auguste

Renoir. The executive chef aboard the *Abenteuer*. He's a genius."

Since the man talks about himself in the third person, I'd have to say that the jury's out about whether he's a genius. Narcissist, sure. But genius? I have my doubts.

Naturally, I don't say this out loud. Instead, I apologize. "Sorry, I'm allergic to marshmallows." A slight fib, but the last thing I need is to get on the wrong side of Auguste Renoir. I wouldn't want him to poison my food.

The chef looks at me with disdain. "Peanut allergies, seafood allergies, now marshmallow allergies. What's next? Are people going to start claiming they're allergic to water?" Then he storms into the kitchen, yelling at a sous-chef who didn't peel the carrots to his master's liking.

"Well, shall we get started?" Sophia asks. She spends the next hour explaining the menus, the wine selection, seating arrangements, and table settings. When she starts to show me how the salt and pepper shakers are refilled, I stop her.

"Do you mind if we finish this later?" I check the time on my phone and gulp. "I have less than twenty-one hours to memorize everything in this binder."

"Don't forget the welcome presentation you have to give tomorrow evening," Sophia says.

"Welcome presentation?"

"Yes, after dinner, the tour manager gives a two-hour presentation to the passengers. It's considered one of the highlights of the cruise." Sophia smiles bitterly. "Or at least it was when Maria had the job."

I put my head in my hands and groan. "I hate public speaking."

"Maria loved it."

"Of course she did," I say. "It probably helped that she knew what she was talking about. I don't have a clue."

Sophia's expression softens. "Maria and I shared a cabin. I think she may have left her flash drive behind. It might have the presentation she used for the welcome session on it. I'll check when I get off duty."

"I'd really appreciate that," I say.

"No problem." Sophia walks to the kitchen and pushes on the swinging door with her hip. She motions at my legs. "Better make sure you're wearing nylons next time Frau Albrecht sees you. I wouldn't want you to get fired."

As she walks into the kitchen and calls out for Auguste Renoir, I wonder why Sophia is suddenly being so helpful. One minute she's angry that I got the tour manager job instead of her. Now she wants to make sure I don't get fired? Something fishy is going on aboard this boat, and it's not just the salmon they're serving for dinner.

* * *

As Erich and I walk through the old town of Mainz to the restaurant later that night, he refuses to explain the mission until after we eat.

"You'll be able to think more clearly on a full stomach," he says to me. "You know how you get when your blood sugar levels drop."

I stop in the middle of the picturesque market square and put my hands on my hips. "Exactly how do I get?"

Erich waves a hand in my direction. "Like this. Cranky."

"I'm not cranky."

"If you say so."

I step forward and jab my finger in Erich's chest. "I *do* say so. Besides, how would you know anything about my blood sugar levels, anyway?"

"Your file was very extensive." Erich gives me a sly smile. "Do you want me to tell you what it says about what you talk about in your sleep?"

My jaw drops. "Please tell me you're kidding."

"I am. The only person who would know if you talk in your sleep or not is your boyfriend."

"I don't have a boyfriend," I say. "But I suppose you already knew that."

Instead of responding, Erich grabs my hand and leads me across the square to a pedestrian street lined with rustic half-timbered buildings. "The restaurant is down here."

I pepper him with more questions about the arms

deal, but he limits his responses to historical tidbits about Mainz.

"Did you know that you're walking through over two thousand years of history? This area dates back to Roman times," Erich says. "And remember the medieval tower we passed by earlier? It's called the Eisenturm, or Iron Tower. It used to be a watchtower and gate on the old city walls."

I'm finding it hard to concentrate on what Erich is saying. And no, it's not because my blood sugar levels are low. Or because Erich is holding my hand.

No, frankly, it's because Erich's history lesson is boring. While my friend, Ginny, would be thrilled to learn that Mainz is where Johannes Gutenberg invented the movable type press, I can't stop yawning.

But when Erich mentions Mainz is the wine capital of Germany, my ears perk up.

"Wine? Yes, please," I say.

As Erich ushers me inside the restaurant, he promises to order us a bottle of his favorite riesling.

The minute I walk into the cozy dining room, I feel like I'm transported back in time. Beeswax candles flicker against the plastered walls, pottery is displayed along wood shelves running the length of the room, and the trestle tables and benches look as though they've been here since the Middle Ages.

A woman wearing a moss green skirt and bodice paired with a white lace blouse and apron seats us in a booth in a secluded alcove. Before I can stop him, Erich orders pfälzer saumagen for both of us.

"I would have preferred to choose for myself," I say. "Maybe I would have liked something else."

"Trust me, you'll love the pfälzer saumagen."

I take a sip of the crisp riesling, then say, "Trust is something you'll have to earn."

"If we're going to work together, you're going to have to trust me." He takes a sip of wine, then leans back against the booth and stares at me, almost as though he's daring me to challenge him.

So I do. "You said 'if' we work together. That means I can walk away from all this and you."

He laughs, which annoys me. "You could, but I suggest you wait, try the pfälzer saumagen, and hear what I have to say first."

I give him my fiercest stare. "Okay, I'm waiting."

"First, we eat. Then we talk."

When the waitress brings our entrees, I ask her what pfälzer saumagen is.

"Pfälzer refers to the region and saumagen means 'sow's stomach' in English," she says. "The stuffing consists of pork, potatoes, onions, and spices."

"Did she say 'stomach'?" I ask after the waitress leaves. "I'm pretty sure any file of mine would have pointed out that I don't eat organ meat."

"Ronald Reagan sampled saumagen when he visited Germany," Erich says.

"And that's supposed to be a selling point?"

Eventually, Erich persuades me to try it, and, between you and me, it is delicious. And the side dishes of mashed potatoes and sauerkraut are so good that I want to lick my plate clean.

When we're finished, Erich asks if I want some strudel for dessert.

"It's not made with kidney or liver is it?"

"No, just apples . . . although if you prefer kidneys and liver, I'm sure that could be arranged."

"Let's stick with apples."

When the strudel arrives, Erich is finally ready to tell me about the mission. I don't know why he had to wait until dessert to spill the beans. Must be some kind of control thing. I've met men like him before—emotionally detached, secretive, and always having to be in charge. In fact, I've dated a guy like that before. Huge mistake.

"So exactly what kind of mission is this?" I ask in between bites of flaky, buttery pastry and juicy, spiced apples.

"The kind where we save the world," Erich says.

"That's a bit overly dramatic, don't you think?"

"I don't do drama. I only do truth."

I roll my eyes. "Slap that slogan on a t-shirt and some coffee mugs, and you'll make a fortune."

"I have no interest in making money. I'm interested in—"

"Yeah, yeah. I know. You're all about saving the world." I push my empty dessert plate aside. "How about some details about this world-saving mission?"

"We have intelligence that an international arms deal is going to take place in Basel, Switzerland."

"You do realize that we're in Mainz, Germany, right? Basel is what, like two hundred miles away?"

Erich smiles. "Someone's been studying their binder."

"I wish you hadn't mentioned the binder," I say. "I've wasted over two hours here with you, hours that I could have used to study."

"Isabelle, your IQ is off the charts and you have a photographic memory. All you have to do is skim through the binder and you'll be all set."

"It's not quite that simple." I look longingly at Erich's unfinished strudel, and he pushes his plate toward me. "Tell me more about the mission. All I know is that the deal takes place in Basel."

"See, you are a quick study. I said that five seconds ago and you've retained that information like that." Erich snaps his fingers.

I ignore his barb. "But on this cruise, we're not headed to Basel. We're headed north to Amsterdam."

"That's true."

"Then why am I involved?"

"Because a jewel thief is going to be one of your passengers."

I arch an eyebrow. "I thought this was about illegal weapons, not jewelry."

Erich takes a sip of his espresso, then says, "It's

about both. The jewel thief has a stolen emerald necklace—"

"Obviously it's stolen," I point out. "You're talking about a jewel thief."

"See, what did I say about you being smart?" Erich represses a smile, then adds, "The jewel thief is going to sell the necklace to a fence in Amsterdam. The fence will then sell the necklace to the head of the Nouveau Rouge Order."

I gasp. "The Nouveau Rouge Order is involved? But they're responsible for . . ." I can't bear to utter out loud the atrocities they've committed.

"Now you see why it's important that this deal is stopped?" Erich fills my wine glass. "Well, the head of the Nouveau Rouge Order is going to, in turn, sell the necklace to a sheikh in exchange for the weapons. That transaction will take place in Basel."

"But no one knows what the head of the Nouveau Rouge Order looks like," I say. "We don't even know if it's a man or a woman. At least that's what they report in the press. Maybe the organization knows more?"

"Well, fortunately, that's not something you have to worry about. You only need to help us with the operation in Amsterdam."

I take a sip of wine and consider what Erich has told me. This riesling really is good. After another sip, I ask, "Why doesn't the jewel thief take a plane to Amsterdam? It seems odd to vacation with a stolen necklace."

"Possibly because security checks aren't as stringent on a riverboat. Or maybe he's afraid of flying," Erich suggests.

"I can relate to the fear of flying." I rub my temples. "I'm starting to get a headache. Do you have any painkillers?"

"You should be careful who you accept pills from," Erich says.

"Why? Because they could be poisoned?"

"It's been known to happen."

"I really hope you're not serious."

Erich reaches across the table and takes my hand in his. "I won't let anything happen to you. That's why I'm on this cruise, to watch out for you."

"So if you're on the cruise, why don't you do all this super secret spy stuff? Not that you've told me what I need to do yet."

"I don't have the necessary skill-set. But you do. Don't worry, what you have to do is simple." Erich squeezes my hand, then releases it. "Just get close to the jewel thief. Make him trust you, gain his confidence, and then . . . well, I'll fill you in on the rest of the details later."

I shake my head. "Later? You can't be serious."

"It's for your own protection," Erich says. "The less you know right now, the better."

"Fine," I say through clenched teeth. "But you can at least tell me why you picked me for this."

"Three reasons. First, your background as an intelligence analyst in the Air Force means you have all the necessary clearances. Second, you already were working on the riverboat the jewel thief will be on. It was a simple matter of pulling strings to get you promoted to a job where you'll have close contact with the jewel thief."

"You might want to explain that to Sophia," I mutter.

Erich taps his finger on the table. "And third, and perhaps most important, you play Scrabble at a championship level."

As if all that wasn't enough to digest, Erich then presents me with a jewelry box. Yeah, cause that's what you do when you're enlisting someone to help save the world—you give them jewelry.

CHAPTER 3
RASH CREAM DISASTERS

The next morning, I get ready for work. After tucking my hair into its regulation bun, I put on my uniform—black skirt and jacket, white blouse, and those dreaded nylons. My legs instantly react, sending signals to my brain that scream, "Scratch us! Now!"

I ignore my legs' demands while I open the velvet box that Erich gave me last night. Ordinarily, I wouldn't accept jewelry from a stranger, but I made an exception in this case. After all, it's for the mission. The fact that I love charm bracelets doesn't hurt either.

Pulling the bracelet out of the box, I marvel at the gold charms—each one is a replica of a Scrabble tile with the various letters and point values etched on them.

I run my fingers over the "E" tile. Funny how it's right next to the "I" tile. "E" for Erich and "I" for Isabelle. When Erich clasped the bracelet on my wrist after dinner, I made a joke about how I can't seem to escape him, not even metaphorically on a charm bracelet. I thought it was funny, but he didn't crack a smile.

"Focus on the mission. The jewel thief is a Scotsman named Hamish MacDougall." Erich showed me a picture of a man in his late sixties or early seventies. His hair is white, but his beard still has a touch of russet. The man had probably been a full-blown redhead when he was younger.

Erich told me that Hamish has been responsible for some of the most notorious jewelry heists in Europe, but that no one has ever been able to prove it. Then he added, "Make sure Hamish notices your bracelet and then you can use it as a way to build rapport with him."

"Why? Is he going to want to steal it?" I asked.

Erich shook his head. "No, this isn't valuable enough for someone like him."

"Then why the bracelet?"

"Because he's obsessed with Scrabble," Erich explained. "When he finds out you're a Scrabble champion, he'll want to play with you. Prove that you're a worthy opponent, someone who can compete at an international level. Then, when the time is right, he'll ask you to be on his team at the Scrabble tournament in Amsterdam."

"That's it? Play Scrabble?"

"Yes. That's it . . . for now," he said as adjusted the bracelet, his fingers stroking the inside of my wrist and sending shivers down my spine.

As I recall the sensation of Erich's touch on my skin, my breath hitches in my chest.

Snap out of it, Isabelle. There wasn't anything romantic about his touch. This is just a job for him.

I tuck some wayward strands of hair back into my bun, then grab my binder. Time to head to the library and get some more studying done before the passengers embark this afternoon.

"You're late, again," Frau Albrecht barks as I walk through the reception area.

I glance at the clock on the wall. "But it's only eight. I don't have to be at the check-in desk until one."

"Correct. But you were supposed to be in the dining room thirty minutes ago."

"Oh, thanks, but I'm not hungry," I reply. "I had a big dinner last night."

"Your lack of appetite isn't my concern," she says. "Your dereliction of duty is."

"Dereliction of duty?" I splutter. "I was awake until three this morning reading about Heidelberg Castle, the Gutenberg Museum, and how riesling wine is made."

"Humph. That explains those dark circles under

your eyes. You know they have concealer for that kind of thing." The older woman presses her lips together as she examines my legs. "Wear some dark-colored nylons to hide that rash."

"The nylons are what's causing the rash," I point out. "If you could make an exception so that I don't have to wear them, then—"

Frau Albrecht slams her hand on the desk. "No more exceptions. It's bad enough that Head Office sent an email saying you should be allowed to wear non-regulation jewelry. All the other women who work aboard this boat are content with a pair of simple stud earrings, but no, you have to wear a gaudy bracelet too."

I take a quick step backwards, conscious of the gold charms swaying back and forth on my wrist. "I'm sorry. I didn't realize they would do that," I say, trying to appease her.

She points toward the hallway leading off the reception area. "Go."

Figuring flight is the better option in this situation, I rush into the dining room.

"Finally." Sophia motions for me to join her at one of the tables. She hands me a stack of napkins. "Fold these."

As I try to follow along while Sophia transforms a napkin into a flower, I ask her why we're doing this.

"This isn't a large ocean-going cruise ship with staff dedicated to certain departments," she says.

"There are only thirty crew members aboard the *Abenteuer.* We all have to pitch in."

"I hope they don't expect me to cook. Unless the passengers like burnt toast, then I'm your girl," I joke.

Sophia narrows her eyes. "I doubt the executive chef would let you in his kitchen. Not after how you insulted his marshmallows. Now hurry up and fold those napkins. We still have to help get cabins ready."

"How long is that going to take? I need to get ready for my welcome presentation."

"Oh, you don't have to worry about that. I found Maria's presentation on her thumb drive." Sophia smiles, but it's one of those smiles that doesn't quite reach the eyes. "All you'll have to do is click through the slides and read off the talking points."

"Wow, really? Thanks a million. You're saving my butt." I continue to work on the napkins, but mine look more like mushrooms than flowers. After trying to fold a few more, Sophia shakes her head and tells me to place wine glasses on each table instead.

Auguste Renoir hovers behind me with a ruler, making sure each glass is placed at the appropriate distance from the edge of the table.

"No, no, no!" The chef throws his hands in the air. "If the table is not set correctly, it will reflect poorly on Auguste Renoir."

After he shouts at me for setting a red wine glass down instead of a white wine glass, I stamp my foot. "Isabelle Martinez cannot work in these conditions." I shake my head when I realize I've started referring to myself in the third person, too.

The chef puts his hands on his hips. "Then perhaps Isabelle Martinez should quit."

I thrust the wine glass I'm holding at him. "Fine, I will."

"You're going to quit?" Sophia asks hopefully from across the room.

"I am . . ." I pause when I see my charm bracelet reflected in the windowpane. I take a deep breath and continue, "I am *not* going to quit."

Darn that Erich. He's managed to convince me that I'm essential to this mission. If I quit, then the terrorists would win. No matter how much I want to flounce off this riverboat, I can't.

The chef hands me back the wine glass. "Continue. Auguste Renoir doesn't have all day."

After another hour getting the dining room ready, and then another three hours cleaning cabins—turns out my strong suit is cleaning toilet bowls—Sophia and I head down to the reception desk.

"You sit here," she says, motioning at one of the stools. "After I check in each passenger, hand them a welcome packet, make sure they know where their cabin is, and answer any questions they have."

My hands shake as the first people board the boat. What if they ask me difficult questions, like "Which direction does the Rhine River flow?" Or "Do I need an electrical adapter for my hairdryer?"

I'm so nervous that I'm worried that the hives on my legs are going to start spreading to my arms and face. That would not be a good look. But what would be worse is if Hamish MacDougall rebuffs my attempts to bond with him.

I listen carefully to people's accents as Sophia checks them in. There are plenty of German, Swedish, and French accents, but no one speaks with a Scottish lilt. One couple converses rapidly with Sophia in Greek. I wonder what she's said to them about me because when I hand them their welcome packets, they look at me like I have the plague.

My ears perk up when I hear fellow Americans. "Hello there, darling," a middle-aged woman says to Sophia. "We're the Sinclairs. Emma and Hank Sinclair."

"I'm Hank and she's Emma," her husband points out.

Emma playfully slaps Hank's arm. "She can figure that out, silly. Why would a gal as good-looking as me be named Hank?"

I lean forward. "Where are you from?"

"Alabama," Emma says.

"Greenville, Alabama," Hank adds.

I grin. "That's near where *Sweet Home Alabama* took place, right? I loved that movie."

"Me too." Emma smiles. "Do I sense a little southern in that accent of yours?"

"Yes, ma'am," I say. "Texas born and bred."

Emma looks at Hank. "And you thought there wouldn't be any Americans aboard this cruise."

Sophia kicks my leg under the desk, causing my hives to cry out again to be scratched. "Stop chitchatting," she says in an undertone. "There's a line of people waiting to check in."

After telling the Sinclairs that I'll see them later, Sophia and I continue working. We have two hundred passengers on this cruise, which is significantly smaller than what you'll find on a big ocean-going cruise ship. It means that we can get to know the passengers on a more personal level, and more importantly for the mission, I can keep a close eye on Hamish. That is, if he ever shows up.

After an hour has passed and there's no one else waiting in line, Sophia says, "Looks like that's everyone accounted for."

"Are you sure?" I furrow my brow. "Where's the—" I stop myself just in time. Can you imagine if I had asked Sophia where the jewel thief was?

"Where's the what?" Sophia asks without looking up from her keyboard.

"The maps of the boat," I say to cover my tracks. "I seem to have misplaced them."

Before Sophia can answer, an older gentleman shuffles toward the check-in desk. He's leaning heavily on an intricately carved cane, and each step he takes looks painful. "Good afternoon, lassies," he calls out cheerfully.

I mentally pull up Hamish MacDougall's picture in my head. Yep, this is him. The notorious jewel thief. The man who is going to be indirectly responsible for terrorists getting their hands on illegal weapons.

Extending my hand so that he'll notice my Scrabble charm bracelet, I start to say hello, but Sophia bats my arm away. "You're out of welcome packets," she says. "Go grab another one from the back."

By the time I find the spare packets—they were hidden underneath Frau Albrecht's enormous purse—Sophia is already directing Hamish to the elevator. "Just take that up one flight to your cabin," she says.

I try to rush after him to give his welcome packet, but Sophia tells me not to bother. "I found one already."

My shoulders slump. I missed my opportunity to connect with Hamish. It's only day one of the cruise and I've already botched the mission.

* * *

After finishing my shift, I head to my quarters, grateful that I have a single room. Sophia had cattily pointed out that this was unusual for someone at my job level.

"The only reason I have my own room right now is because Maria used to be my roommate," she told me. "And now Maria is gone. Transferred because of you."

Did Erich arrange for me to get my own room? He's pulled strings already—engineering my tour manager promotion and getting an exception to the dress code so that I can wear this charm bracelet—maybe the single cabin is also his work. Now, if only he could get Frau Albrecht to drop the nylons requirement.

Earlier this afternoon, she gave me a pair of black nylons to hide my rash. They're even itchier than my previous ones. I have a couple of hours before I'm back on duty, so I strip off my uniform and take a cool shower, hoping that will soothe my legs.

It doesn't help. My legs are wet, but they still feel like they're on fire. I slip on my robe, comb my hair, then perch on the edge of the lower bunk. After sending my friend Ginny a quick text, I slather rash cream on my legs.

While I'm screwing the lid back on the rash cream container, a knock on the door startles me. When I drop the container, I utter a naughty word, possibly two. All of my rash cream is on the floor. Who knows when I'll be able to get more.

I sigh. Please let the person who knocked be a rash cream salesperson. I stand and walk over to the door, but before I can open it, Erich walks in.

"Uh, hello," I say sarcastically. "Most people wait to be invited into someone's cabin before they enter."

"Didn't you say come in?" Erich asks.

"No, I said . . . never mind." I grab a towel from the bathroom and start to clean up the rash cream from the floor.

"Sorry," he says. "Good thing I'm not a vampire."

"Huh?"

"Vampires can't enter someone's home unless they're invited. Didn't you see *Twilight*?"

"I'm sure my file was very clear about the fact that I can't stand sci-fi and fantasy movies." As I wipe up the rest of the rash cream, I say, "But it's a relief to know that you don't sleep in a coffin at night."

"No, coffins are too constraining. I toss and turn when I'm sleeping."

My face grows warm as I imagine what Erich looks like tossing and turning in bed. Is he the type of guy who wears a t-shirt and shorts to sleep in? Or pajamas? In the buff?

Oh my gosh, I have to stop thinking about Erich in this way. I turn to him and snap, "What are you doing here, anyway?"

"I'm here for your debriefing. Standard operating procedure after an agent makes contact with a target." Erich unbuttons his jacket and sits down on my bunk. "So what did you find out about our Hamish MacDougall?"

"Nothing. Sophia didn't give me a chance to speak with him." I tuck my hair behind my ears, then groan. "Great. Now I have rash cream in my hair."

Erich looks at my legs. "You really should see a doctor about that."

"Better yet, why don't you get Frau Albrecht to

drop the nylons requirement?"

"I tried, believe me, but my contact in Head Office can only do so much. If he asks for too many exceptions, people would become suspicious."

I walk into the bathroom, saying over my shoulder, "Oh, come on, nylons are the least suspicious thing you could request. Promoting someone like me on the spot to a tour manager position? That's what sends up red flags."

After I wash the rash cream out of my hair, I run a brush through it. When I come back out, Erich says, "You look nice with your hair down."

"Yeah, that's another thing your guy could work on—getting rid of the bun requirement. The pins hurt my head."

Erich holds my gaze for a moment, then clears his throat. "We should get back to the debrief."

"I told you, I don't have any information to share," I say. "I didn't speak with the jewel thief."

"That doesn't mean you don't have any intel." Erich stands and crosses the short distance in the room to face me. Placing his hands on my shoulders, he says, "You'll have learned something about Hamish MacDougall without realizing it. Somewhere in that subconscious of yours is valuable information."

I gasp when Erich spins me around and places his hands over my eyes, messing up my hair in the process. "Relax, take a few deep breaths, and cast your mind back to when you first saw the jewel thief."

Exactly how am I supposed to relax in this situation? Erich is inches away from me. When I squirm, he whispers, "Keep your eyes closed. It will help you recall important details. Think back. Shutting off your vision will help awaken your memories. What are your other senses telling you?"

This is torture. Complete and utter torture. The only thing I can sense is Erich. The feel of his hands on my face, the smell of his cologne, the taste of his lips.

Whoa, hang on there, buttercup. It's not like you've kissed Erich. How would you know how his lips taste?

"This is ridiculous," I mutter.

"Humor me, Isabelle. Just relax and tell me the first thing that comes to mind."

"If I do, will you leave me in peace?"

"Of course," he says. "Now, deep breaths in, deep breaths out."

As I inhale and exhale slowly, I feel him doing the same. Soon we're breathing in sync, like it's the most natural thing in the world.

"The jewel thief," Erich prompts.

"His cane looks like an antique, but it's a fake. There's a slight groove where the ivory handle meets the ebony wood. He's originally from Aberdeenshire, but currently lives in Glasgow. He has a small scar on his left earlobe. Likely from having an earring torn out of his ear. And he recently petted a miniature poodle."

I feel like Sherlock Holmes gleaning all this information from careful observation of Hamish's appearance and listening to his accent.

"Excellent," Erich says crisply. He drops his hands and steps away from me. My senses are shaken from the abrupt way he took his hands off my shoulders. Even though I know he's only a few feet away from me, it feels like he's a million miles away.

When I spin around, he has his hand on the door handle.

"You're leaving?"

"Of course. We finished the debriefing."

"But I . . ." I wring my hands as my voice trails off. I can't very well say that I want him to stay.

Misinterpreting my hesitation, Erich says, "Don't worry. You're doing fine. You're a natural at this. You're going to be a very effective agent for the organization." Then he bows his head slightly before closing the door behind him.

* * *

I rush into the corridor after Erich. "What do you mean by that?" I yell at his retreating back. His only response is a brief wave over his shoulder.

I clench my fists and stomp my feet. Very mature, I know.

I spin around, realizing the door across the hall from me is open. Sophia pokes her head out and asks,

"What is going on out here?"

Cinching my robe tightly around my waist, I turn and apologize. "Sorry, I didn't realize I was speaking so loud."

"Is that who I think it is?" Sophia points toward the end of the corridor where Erich is pushing open the door that leads to the stairwell. She gasps. "If Frau Albrecht finds out you're having an affair with a passenger, she'll fire you."

"An affair? Hah. You'd have to pay me to sleep with that man."

"He's paying you for sex?" Sophia gasps. "That would make you a—"

My eyes widen. "What? No way. I'm not a . . ." I can't bring myself to say the word. I hold up my hands, take a deep breath, then say, "There's nothing going on between the two of us."

Sophia smirks. "Do you always receive male company in your cabin wearing a robe? And your hair looks like the very definition of bed-head."

"Erich showed up unannounced and barged into my cabin. If I had known he was coming—which I didn't—I would have been dressed."

"Erich? Is that what you're calling him?" Sophia cocks her head to one side. "You're on a first-name basis with a VIP passenger and you have the audacity to claim that there's nothing going on."

"Really, there isn't," I say.

"Then why was he in your cabin?"

"Um . . . to give me some rash cream for my legs?"

"Right. Herr Zimmermann just happens to carry around rash cream in his suitcase. Totally believable."

"I think he's a pharmaceutical sales representative. It's a new product that they're doing a clinical trial for." As the words rush out, I realize how unbelievable it all sounds.

"You realize that most clinical trials are done at doctors' offices or hospitals," Sophia points out. "People don't take riverboat cruises to find test subjects."

"They don't?"

"You're a really bad liar. If you're going to have an affair with a passenger, then you should come up with a better cover story." Sophia shakes her head. "Well, I guess it doesn't matter. Once I tell Frau Albrecht about you and Herr Zimmermann, you'll be history. She'll march you off the boat so fast your head will spin."

And I'll have your tour manager job. She leaves this last bit unsaid, but we all know that's what she's thinking.

Sophia startles when a voice says behind us, "Where are the towels, cherie? Auguste Renoir is dripping water all over the floor."

When I spin around, I bite back a smile. The executive chef is standing in Sophia's doorway, buck naked except for his chef's hat and a washcloth that he's holding over his private parts.

"Hmm . . . I seem to recall that as part of my new employee orientation, Frau Albrecht was very clear that the staff is not to engage in, um, what did she call it? Oh, yeah, inappropriate relations with each other." I point at the chef. "Do you think she would consider this inappropriate?"

Sophia grits her teeth. "Fine, let's call a truce. You don't tell her about Auguste and I won't tell her about Herr Zimmermann."

"It's a deal."

Sophia mutters something to the executive chef about being more discreet, then slams the door in my face. After a moment, she opens it back up and hisses. "Better not count on getting Maria's presentation from me. You'll have to wing it."

CHAPTER 4
AN UNEXPECTED PHONE CALL

I have a serious situation on my hands. I was counting on having Maria's presentation. I'd click through her slides, read off her talking points, and try to avoid any detailed questions. Easy peasy. Now I have less than an hour before I'm supposed to be in the lounge to welcome the passengers.

Why did I blackmail Sophia into keeping my supposed affair with Erich a secret? Who cares if she had told Frau Albrecht that I was sleeping with a passenger. Frau Albrecht would have fired me and then I would have been off the hook for this presentation.

Well, there's a perfectly good explanation for that. Two actually. First off, I care about my reputation. The last thing I want is for people to think I was fired because I was having "inappropriate relations" with a VIP passenger. Second, I'm still broke. After telling my mom that I didn't need her financial help after all, I can't really go back and ask for money now.

I let out a huge sigh. Then I leaf through my binder, scrawling notes down furiously while keeping an eye on the time. With only ten minutes to spare, I quickly get dressed and fix my hair and make-up. I run up the two flights of stairs that lead from the lower deck, where the crew cabins are located, up to the reception area. As I'm rounding the corner, ready to dart up the next set of stairs to the lounge, I spot Frau Albrecht at the reception desk. She's cracking her knuckles while barking orders at a hapless desk clerk.

Not wanting to be her next victim, I spin around. I creep backwards out the door onto the outer deck.

"Hey, watch where you're going," someone says, but it's too late. I trip over a coiled rope. As I land on my hands and knees, my binder goes flying out of my arms. It bounces off the deck, sending all my handwritten notes up into the air. I scramble to catch them, but they float off in the breeze and land in the water.

I watch in horror as the pages float off down the Rhine River. Perhaps the passengers would be interested in seeing me do magic tricks instead of giving a welcome presentation? I sigh, then scoop up what's left of my binder. When I walk back into the reception area, Frau Albrecht frowns.

"You're always late," she says. "The passengers will be getting impatient."

I nod, then slowly march up the stairs to my impending doom. The good news is that I scraped my legs when I fell, so the pain from the cuts on my calves is distracting me from the itchiness of my rash. It's important to be able to look on the positive side of things, right?

When I walk into the lounge, I gulp. So many people, all waiting for me. Contrary to what Frau Albrecht said, they don't seem to be waiting impatiently. They're happily sipping on after-dinner drinks, taking selfies, and chatting with their fellow passengers. The room is buzzing with energy. Maybe they won't notice if I silently disappear.

I inch out of the room, being careful this time to look behind me, when someone calls out my name. Emma from Alabama waves at me, then tugs on her husband's sleeve to alert him to my presence. When Hank sees me, he beams.

"Quiet down, folks," he says. "Miss Isabelle is here to give us her presentation."

I look down at my grandmother's amethyst ring. *She was a strong woman. You're a strong woman. You can do this.*

I walk up to the front of the room and grip the sides of the podium. "Good evening, everyone."

"We can't hear you," someone yells from the back.

"Speak up, lassie," another man says.

I look up sharply, recognizing that Scottish accent. Hamish MacDougall is seated at a table in the back of the room. He gives me an encouraging thumbs up.

One of the bartenders rushes up and clips a microphone on the lapel of my jacket. "Is that better?" I ask, checking the sound level with the crowd.

When they murmur their approval, I take a few deep breaths. *You can do this, Isabelle. You've read the binder front to back. The information is in your brain. You just have to let it out.*

I decide to be honest with the audience. "I'm not very good at public speaking," I confess. "In fact, I'm a bundle of nerves."

Being vulnerable seems to work. I can feel supportive energy emanating from the audience. Feeling encouraged, I state the obvious. "You're on board the *Abenteuer*. It's a riverboat."

"I think you mean *she's* a riverboat," someone says. "Boats are always female."

"Yeah, that's true," an older man standing by the bar says. "Like women, ships are unpredictable."

After the crowd good-naturedly boos him, I continue with some other obvious facts. "We're going to sail on the Rhine River and see lots of interesting stuff. There will be delicious food. Did you enjoy your dinner tonight?"

A few of the passengers nod. Others look confused,

like I'm a stand-up comedian who can't seem to deliver a funny punch line.

"Better get on with it, dear," Hank says in a stage whisper. "The crowd is getting restless."

"Um . . . who likes cuckoo clocks?" I ask.

A few people raise their hands.

"There's a place that sells them in, um . . ." I wipe sweat off my brow as I struggle to remember the name of the German town where the shop is.

When I pause to take a sip of water, Sophia approaches the podium. She hands me a laptop. "Here's Maria's presentation," she whispers.

I furrow my brow. "Why the change of heart?"

"It's not about you," she says. "It's about the passengers. They deserve a first-class presentation, not whatever this is that you're doing."

She hooks up the laptop, and I breathe a sigh of relief when Maria's opening slide displays on the screen. I click to the next slide and practically do a fist pump when a map of the Rhine River appears. It triggers my memory, and I point at the screen. "That's Rudesheim. That's where you can buy a cuckoo clock."

"Just read out the talking points on each slide and you'll be fine," Sophia says in an undertone. "Do not ad-lib."

So I do. I talk through the itinerary and explain the optional excursions in each port. The information flows freely. I even start to add in detail to augment

Maria's talking points. I've got this. When I get to a slide titled, "Entertainment on Board," I get a little cocky. I can recite all the activities planned for the passengers from heart. So I simply click to the next slide but don't bother to turn around to look at it.

I start to tell the passengers about the traditional dance troupe who will be performing later in the week when a woman points at the screen and screams.

"What is that?" someone asks.

"It looks like a laboratory experiment," a man says. "Something you'd see in a petri dish."

Other people start to chime in, clearly horrified by what's behind me. When I spin around to see what's so disgusting, I'm confronted with a close-up of a red, blistering rash. A very familiar rash. The very same rash that's on my legs. How do I know it's my rash? Because it says so in big letters right on the slide.

* * *

Could I be any more mortified? I want nothing more than to run out of this room as fast as I can. But for some reason, my feet feel like they're super-glued to the floor. I can't seem to budge.

This is one of those times that I wished alien abduction was real. If little green men beamed me up to their spaceship right now, I'd be thrilled. Who cares if they do some weird experiments on me? It'd be better than being here in a room full of people staring at a picture of the horrifying rash on my legs.

The aliens aren't coming to save the day, are they? My therapist had suggested using humor to manage my anxiety in stressful situation. I clear my throat, then tell a joke. "A friend of mine made so many rash decisions, he became a dermatologist."

I don't know what the bartender is putting in people's drinks, but it must be pretty potent because everyone cracks up. Then, before I know it, people are shouting out their own bad jokes.

When Hank yells out, "How do you spot a secret agent? Give him measles," I look around the room. Is Erich here? Would he laugh at a joke about secret agents? I doubt it.

After a few more minutes of audience participation, I finally manage to wrap things up, telling the passengers to be ready bright and early the next morning for our excursion to Heidelberg Castle.

Several people come up afterwards. Some ask questions about the itinerary, some want to know if the marshmallows are gluten-free. But a surprising number share their own skin condition stories. It's amazing how people can bond over their dermatological issues.

"Honey, my nephew is a dermatologist in Boulder," one lady says. "Why don't I send him pictures of your rash? Then you can do one of those video calls so that you can get his professional opinion. He's single, you know."

I politely thank her, but decline the offer for both the consultation and fix-up. Spotting Hamish at the bar, I rush over to see if I can strike up a conversation with him, but he leaves before I get a chance.

Frau Albrecht's voice booms over the loudspeakers. "Isabelle Martinez, please report to reception."

This should be fun. When I reach the bottom of the stairs, Frau Albrecht is standing there, her arms folded across her chest.

"Head Office phoned," she says. "About you. Again."

"Listen, I can explain," I say. "Sophia gave me those slides. You can't possibly think that I'd show pictures like that."

The older woman furrows her brow. "Pictures of what?"

"Oh, isn't that why Head Office called you?"

"No, they called to say that you don't need to wear nylons anymore." She cracks a couple knuckles, then adds, "Yet another exception is being made for you. Curious, isn't it? What makes you so special?"

Sophia walks out of the back room. "Oh, Isabelle, how did your presentation go?" she asks innocently.

"I think you know exactly how it went," I say. "You sabotaged it."

Sophia holds a hand to her chest. "Me? Never."

Frau Albrecht looks back and forth between the two of us. "What exactly happened during the presentation?"

"I have no idea," Sophia says. "I was in the back room filling out paperwork."

I fling my hands in the air. I've had enough of this. Erich can nab the jewel thief on his own. "Tell you what, Frau Albrecht, why don't I make things easier and resign. It's obvious I'm not wanted here."

At my announcement that I'm quitting, Frau Albrecht gives me a self-satisfied smile. The way she licks her sharp, pointy teeth reminds me of a lioness who is about to devour her kill.

"I'll be sure to inform Head Office of your resignation," she says. "No need to work your two-week notice period. Sophia can take over your job immediately. Why don't you go pack your bags? I'll call for a taxi to collect you."

I sense Erich behind me, and my whole body tenses. He places his hands lightly on my shoulders, then says to Frau Albrecht, "Isabelle isn't resigning."

The older woman presses her lips together. She's obviously in a difficult situation. Contradicting a VIP passenger and personal friend of the cruise ship line owner would be frowned upon by Head Office. But she desperately wants to be rid of me.

What to do, what to do, she seems to be thinking. Her eyes flicker back and forth.

Erich doesn't give her a chance to decide. "Like I

said, Isabelle isn't resigning."

He presses his fingers into my shoulders and says in an undertone that only I can hear, "That was a foolish thing to do."

"What was foolish was agreeing to your ridiculous plan in the first place," I whisper.

There's no response from him. The only sound I can hear is my heart beating. Or is that his heart beating?

Erich suddenly releases me, then says brightly to Frau Albrecht, "I'm glad we cleared that up. Have a good evening."

"Good evening, sir," the older woman says, her voice choking back rage.

"Come along." Erich grabs my elbow and steers me up to the sun deck. The deck chairs are deserted. The passengers are probably all still in the lounge, telling each other jokes and comparing eczema treatments.

Erich comes to a halt at the stern of the boat. He pulls his phone out and places a call. "It's me," he says. "Isabelle needs to be convinced about her importance to this mission. I think it's time we told her everything."

Erich listens intently for a few moments, then brusquely hands me the phone. When I press it to my ear, a familiar voice says gruffly, "Hello, Isabelle."

I'm so startled that I almost drop the phone. The last person I expected to hear on the other end of the line was my former commanding officer. "General

Taylor," I splutter, instantly feeling my posture straightening. I resist the urge to salute.

"It's time you were read in," the general says. "Erich can explain the details more fully, but suffice it to say, this mission is critical. The terrorists' target is the United Nations in New York. If you don't help, there will be a tremendous loss of life. In order for this mission to be successful, Erich needs you. Your country needs you. The world needs you. You need to step up."

The general continues talking, but all I hear repeating over and over through my head is, "Erich needs you." As I stare into his icy-blue eyes, I wonder what it would be like to be truly needed by this man.

CHAPTER 5
A SEMI-NAKED MAN

The next morning, I wake up with an excruciating headache. This sort of thing happens to me when I'm stressed. Considering the fact that I agreed to help Erich and the general save the world, you could say that I'm feeling a bit of pressure.

I squeeze my eyes shut and rub my temples. This can't be real, right? I must be having one of those waking dreams. A dream so vivid that it seems real. Cause there's no way that the United States government has asked me to go undercover and help the German equivalent of James Bond stop an arms deal and prevent a terrorist attack on the United Nations. Sure, that's totally believable.

Nope, here's what's going to happen. I'll open my eyes and find myself lying in bed in my cramped studio apartment in Texas. I'll pop a couple of painkillers, take a shower, put on jeans and a t-shirt, and head to the mini-mart for my shift. I definitely won't be on a riverboat docked on the Rhine River.

I pry my eyes open and . . . whoa, this isn't my apartment. Am I still dreaming? I sit up on the edge of my bed.

Wait a minute, not my bed. My bed is a fold-out couch from Lou's second-hand store. But I appear to be perched on the bottom bunk in a ship's cabin.

The pressure in my head intensifies. You don't feel pain in your dreams, do you? Oh, my gosh, this *is* real. I am working undercover on a riverboat. And that German James Bond? He's real too.

Memories of last night flood back. Erich calling my former commanding officer, General Taylor. The general convincing me that my government needs me. Me reluctantly agreeing to help Erich save the world. Then Erich telling me I should be grateful to him because I don't have to wear nylons anymore.

Okay, time to stop thinking about Erich. Gotta get up and do this tour manager thing. I get ready in record time, probably because I'm not having to spend ten minutes applying rash cream and gingerly pulling nylons on. Actually, I'm tempted to wear nylons just so Erich doesn't have a reason to smugly tell me how he pulled strings and "saved" me from them.

There you go. I'm thinking about him again. Why is

that man always on my mind? He's everything I can't stand—secretive, unemotional, and way too sure of himself.

I check the time. Yikes, I'm late. A quick glance in the mirror to make sure all my hair is tucked into a tight bun, then I dash up to the reception area. I spend the next twenty minutes making sure all the passengers who signed up for the excursion to Heidelberg Castle are on the tour bus. Just as I'm about to tell the driver to close the door, Sophia barges on the bus.

"You're not coming with us, are you?" I ask her. "I thought you were working at the reception desk today."

Sophia ignores me—she's still irritated that her plan to sabotage my presentation last night backfired. Instead of the passengers complaining about me, they're talking about how refreshing it is to have a tour manager who is self-effacing and has a sense of humor.

My nemesis looks around the bus, then says to someone standing outside, "No problem, there's an empty seat." Then she gives me an evil look and says, "Last minute addition to the tour."

Then Erich boards the bus. Super. Just when I thought I was going to get a day away from him.

"Where's Hamish?" he whispers as he sits next to me.

"He canceled at the last minute. Something about

not feeling well."

Erich shoots me a look. "But this tour is supposed to be an opportunity for you to bond with him."

"What was I supposed to do? Tell Frau Albrecht that I can't escort the group to Heidelberg Castle, then barge into Hamish's cabin and force feed him chicken noodle soup until he feels better?"

Erich shakes his head, then stares out the window at the passing scenery.

When the bus pulls up to the historic site, the group oohs and aahs over the picturesque red sandstone edifice. Situated on the forested slopes of the Königstuhl hill, the castle towers over the city of Heidelberg. Over a million people visit this area each year. Fortunately, I'm only responsible for the thirty-two passengers who signed up for this excursion. My duties today consist primarily of babysitting the group. A professional tour guide is going to show them the castle, which is great, because I haven't had a lot of time to study up on the history of the area.

After I hand my group off to the tour guide, a blonde woman in her mid-twenties intercepts me. "You must be Isabelle," she says. "I'm Zoe."

I cock my head to one side, trying to place her. I don't recognize her from the riverboat. Maybe she works at the castle.

"You know, Zoe Randolph," she says. "From the magazine?"

"The magazine?"

"Uh-huh. We're here for the photo shoot. Didn't Sophia tell you we'd be meeting you at the castle?"

"Ah, that explains it." I smile. "Let's just say that Sophia's not great with communication. You're going to have to fill me in."

"No problem. Let me get my colleague over here first." She waves at a man who's standing by the entrance. As he saunters over, he pauses to take a picture of some passengers from the *Abenteuer* who are inspecting the German Renaissance architecture.

Zoe introduces us. "This is Max Guerrero, the magazine's photographer."

Max takes my hand in his and kisses the back of it in a show of exaggerated gallantry. "Pleasure to meet you, Isabelle."

Zoe rolls her eyes. "Max, knock it off. We're here to do a job, not find you a girlfriend."

Max grins. "Who says I can't do both?"

"Just ignore him. I find it works better that way," Zoe says to me. "Anyway, we were sent here by a travel magazine to do a story on the riverboat cruise."

Max holds up his camera. "I'm in charge of the pictures. Zoe takes care of the words."

"That's because you can barely string a sentence together," Zoe says to him. "Taking photos is the easy part. All you have to do is point and click."

"There's way more to it than that. You have to consider the lighting and camera angles. Then there's the post-production editing." Max turns to me and pretends to frame up a shot. "In the case of Isabelle, she's so gorgeous that I wouldn't need to worry about lighting or do any editing."

Zoe makes a gagging motion. "Enough already, Casanova. Why don't you go take some photos while Isabelle and I talk logistics."

Max gives her a playful salute, then goes off to join the tour group.

"Sorry about my colleague. He's a compulsive flirter." Her smile fades for a moment, then she says brightly, "Fortunately, he doesn't behave that way with me. We keep things professional."

We talk for a while about arranging interviews with some of the passengers, then Zoe says, "Who's that guy? He keeps staring at you."

I look over in the direction she's indicating and see Erich. His arms are folded across his chest, a sour expression is on his face, and his gaze fixed firmly on me. The total opposite of fun-loving, flirtatious Max. "Oh, him. He's a VIP passenger."

"Is there anything between you two?" Zoe asks. "He's got that possessive vibe going on. You should have seen the look on his face when Max was flirting with you."

I press my lips together. "Nope, nothing going on. It's strictly professional."

"If you say so." Zoe looks dubious. "I better go check on Max and make sure he's taking photos, not chatting up girls."

After she walks off, I turn to look back at Erich. We engage in a staring contest for a few moments. Man, could he look any crankier? I take a photo of him to send to one of my friends. I had sent her a text earlier about meeting a mysterious stranger and she wants to see what he looks like.

While I'm checking to see how the picture turned out, Erich grabs my phone. "No photos of me."

"Hey, that's personal property," I say, yanking it back.

"I don't like having my picture taken," Erich says.

"I don't like marshmallows, but that doesn't mean I can stop other people from eating them."

"A picture is different."

"How?"

"A marshmallow is just . . ."

"A disgusting, sugary treat?" I suggest.

He nods. "They really are disgusting, aren't they? How can people eat them?"

I shrug. "No accounting for taste. But why do you care if I take your picture? Are you worried I'm going to steal your image and do some voodoo over it?"

Erich furrows his brow. "Voodoo?"

"You know, a magic spell to make you do something you don't want to do."

"Like kiss you?"

My mouth drops open. "Where did that come from?"

"Just seeing if it would get a reaction out of you."

There's zero emotion in his voice, which infuriates me for some reason. "I definitely do not want you to kiss me."

"I see," he says calmly.

"I think we should change the subject." I tug at my jacket. "Why do you hate having your picture taken? It's not like you're hideous looking."

"You think I'm good-looking?"

"I didn't say that. I said you're *not* hideous looking. That's the bottom of the scale. The next step up is 'horrible,' followed by 'ugly.' Good-looking is near the top of the scale."

"So, which one am I? Horrible or ugly?"

"Let me take another picture and we'll see."

"No pictures," he says intently. "In my line of work, we avoid pictures."

I wave my hands at the crowd of tourists milling about. "You don't think you're in a million people's pictures already in the background?"

"Probably," he says. "But their phones are less likely to be monitored. You're part of this mission. You have to be careful."

"So is it okay if I look at cute kitten videos?" I ask sarcastically.

"I'm not really a fan of kittens," Erich says. "Puppies would be okay."

"Hmm, and here's me thinking pythons were more your thing."

Max comes over and interrupts us. "Sorry, man, I

just need to ask Isabelle something." He turns to me and drapes his arm over my shoulders. "Would you be able to show me around the ship later today as part of my photo shoot?"

"The ship isn't that big," Erich says. "You can find your way around on your own."

Max steps away from me and turns to face Erich straight on. As the two guys square off I notice that, although Max is taller, Erich's shoulders are broader. Not that broad shoulders are a thing for me. They aren't. Really.

Trying to calm things down, I put my hand on Erich's arm and give it a gentle squeeze. Then I turn to Max. "No problem. I'll meet you after dinner?"

Max gives Erich a cocky grin, then rejoins the tour group.

Erich looks down at my hand, and I quickly remove it. "You need to stay focused on the mission," he says. "You can flirt with guys once it's over."

"I wasn't flirting with Max."

"Yes, you were. You batted your eyes at him."

"Batted my eyes? What era are you from?" I laugh while I do an exaggerated batting of my eyes. "Like this? Sounds like you're jealous."

"Jealous? No. I'm a professional. The only reason I'm interested in your love life is because of the mission."

Man, is this guy tense. He takes everything so seriously. When I ask him if he ever relaxes, he says,

"Sure, in between missions."

"When's the last time you were between missions?"

Erich considers this for a moment, then says quietly, "I can't remember."

"Pretend you had a day off from saving the world. What would you do?"

Erich frowns. "That's a silly question."

I put my hand back on his arm and, this time, he doesn't seem to care. "Just humor me. What would you do if you had twenty-four hours of uninterrupted time where you didn't have to worry about anything but you?"

"I'd go horseback riding."

"You like horses? I grew up with them. We have a ranch and I . . ." I hold up my hand. "Why am I telling you that? Of course, you already know about my family's ranch. You know, it really sucks knowing everything about me is in some file."

"That's not true, Isabelle." Erich's gaze softens. "All your thoughts are secret. No one knows what you're thinking except you."

He excuses himself, and as he walks away, I chew on my lip. Thank goodness he doesn't know what goes on in my head. Cause if he did, he'd know that I can't stop thinking about kissing him.

* * *

By the time I get all the passengers back to the boat from Heidelberg Castle, I'm exhausted. Who knew that babysitting a group of tourists was so tiring? Erich disappeared halfway through the tour, telling me he'd find his own way back to the boat. I was having a hard time being around him without thinking extremely unprofessional thoughts, so I was grateful that he left.

I head to the kitchen to grab a sandwich for dinner, planning to eat in my room and study up on our next destination.

"There you are," the executive chef says when I walk through the door. "Herr Zimmermann has requested room service, and he wants you to bring it to his stateroom."

"Me?" I gulp, not wanting to face Erich again today.

"Auguste Renoir does not like that tone of voice." He slams a steak on the counter and glares at me. "Everyone is busy getting the dining room dinner ready for the first seating."

A waitress bustles into the kitchen to grab some glasses. "She thinks she's better than the rest of us," she says. "Gallivants around all day sightseeing, then wants to take the rest of the night off and have a bubble bath while everyone else works."

"Did you know that she doesn't have to wear nylons?" a dishwasher informs the room. "Special exception from Head Office."

The waitress scowls. "Lucky girl. I can't stand wearing nylons."

I hold up my hands. "First, I wasn't sightseeing. Second, I don't have a bathtub. And third . . . well, I agree. Nylons suck. Maybe if all the women banded together and stopped wearing them, Head Office would change the policy."

The chef points to the corner of the kitchen. "Wait there while I finish grilling Herr Zimmermann's steaks."

I furrow my brow. "Steaks? Plural?"

"One of them is probably for you," the waitress says cattily. "He also ordered caviar and champagne."

"Voilà," the chef says as he plates Erich's dinner. "Now go. You are disrupting Auguste Renoir's kitchen."

I grumble the entire time I wheel the cart to Erich's stateroom. The grumbling turns into shallow breathing when Erich opens the door. The man is completely naked. His skin glistens with droplets of water, and he's holding a razor in one hand.

Okay, he's not *completely* naked. There is a towel wrapped around his waist, but I'm pretty sure there's nothing on underneath that. So, yeah, naked.

I push the cart toward him. "Here's your dinner."

Erich steps back and points at the table by the window. "Go ahead and set it up there."

"Um, I think I'll pass." Yep, no way I'm going to go in there with a naked man. "You can leave the cart outside your door when you're done and someone will be by to pick it up."

A couple walks by Erich's stateroom at that very moment, and stops to say hello to him. Erich points at the table again. "Go on," he says to me. "This is room service, isn't it? If I wanted self-service, I would have gone to a fast-food restaurant."

Not wanting the other passengers to witness me flinging a steak at him, I wheel the cart inside. I set the plates and glasses on the table, then set the champagne bucket next to them.

"Go on and sit down," Erich says as he closes the door behind him. "I'll just be a minute."

"Sit?"

"Yes, you know how to sit, don't you? You lower yourself down onto a chair. For someone with an IQ off the charts, you'd think you'd be familiar with the concept."

"Someone's cranky," I say. "Sounds like you might have low blood sugar. Is that why you ordered two steaks?"

"No, I ordered two steaks because there's going to be two people dining."

"Oh . . ." It dawns on me that he probably invited another woman to his stateroom for dinner. I try to recall who among the passengers he might be interested in and all I can come up with is a woman from Luxembourg who I saw him talking with earlier. "Then why do you want me to sit down?"

He shakes his head. "Because you're the woman I'm dining with. Now sit."

I perch on the edge of the chair. Why do I feel relieved that it's me the other steak is for, not the lady from Luxembourg?

A few minutes later, Erich comes out of the bathroom, dressed in gray slacks and a black t-shirt. His hair is still damp, and he's freshly shaven. As he fills up the champagne flutes, he says, "I thought it might be a good idea if we got to know each other better so that we can work more effectively as a team."

"Team-building? Over steak and caviar?"

"Can you think of a better way?"

"Well, at the mini-mart, team-building usually consisted of seeing who could restock the shelves quicker. Whoever lost had to clean the men's room."

Erich smiles briefly, then raises his glass. "How about a toast? Here's to—"

Before he can finish, there's a knock on his door. When Erich opens it, I hear Frau Albrecht greet him. "Good evening, Herr Zimmermann. Since you're a VIP passenger, I wanted to check in and make sure everything is to your satisfaction."

I try to maneuver my chair so that she won't see me, but I'm not quick enough.

"Isabelle, is that you?" Frau Albrecht frowns. "What are you doing in a passenger's cabin?"

Erich comes to my rescue . . . kind of. "I asked

Isabelle to have dinner with me. I want her to give me a personal history lesson of the region."

"Personal?" Frau Albrecht arches an eyebrow at me. "Exactly how personal?"

Before I can answer, Erich says, "Thanks for checking in. Have a good evening." Then he quickly closes the door before she can ask any more questions.

I push back my chair. "I don't think this is a good idea. I think from now on, we should meet in public places. This is ruining my reputation."

"Do you really care what people think of you?" Erich asks.

"Of course I do, don't you?"

"Not really."

"I find that hard to believe."

Erich looks out the window at the water and says slowly, "Maybe there is one person whose opinion I care about."

Could he be talking about me? I rub my grandmother's ring, hoping it will give me some guidance as to how to handle this situation. The answer comes to me with blinding clarity—*Run as fast as you can before you kiss him or he kisses you. You must avoid kissing. Kissing this man would be very, very dangerous.*

"I need to go." I push past Erich and race to the door. Then I say something stupid. "I'm supposed to meet Max."

Erich's eyes turn steely. "We wouldn't want you to be late, would we?"

CHAPTER 6
MYSTERY MEAT

The next day, after an early breakfast, the ship sets sail for Rudesheim, a major tourist attraction in the region. We'll be there until mid-afternoon when we set sail again, traveling through the Rhine Gorge to Koblenz.

Luckily for me, it's a semi-free day. The passengers have a choice of two organized excursions led by professional guides, or they can explore the town on their own. For those folks who are going to do their own thing, I'm responsible for shepherding them from the boat to the center of town. From there, they'll go off and enjoy the shops, restaurants, and historical attractions. Then I'll meet back up with them in the afternoon to make sure they get back before the *Abenteuer* departs.

Hamish didn't sign up for any of the excursions, so I assume he's going to explore the town and I'll finally get my opportunity to speak with him. But when he doesn't appear, I'm at a loss as to what to do. Frau Albrecht is tapping her watch, making it clear I should have left with the group fifteen minutes ago.

"Alright, everyone, let's head into town." Holding up an umbrella so they don't lose sight of me, I lead the passengers from the dock to Drosselgasse, a quaint street in the heart of the old town.

Everyone wanders off except Erich. He's acting like nothing happened last night. No more talk of team building. No more innuendos. He's back to being aloof and business-like. I'm surprised that he isn't giving me a hard time for Hamish being a no-show.

"Don't worry," he says to me. "I heard one of the desk clerks say that he's planning on coming into town a bit later. They've arranged a taxi for him."

"This isn't a huge town, but it's still not going to be easy to track him down," I say.

Erich rubs his hands together. "You're in luck. I know exactly where he'll be. We know that he's a cuckoo clock collector. There's a famous shop that sells them near here that he's bound to visit. All we have to do is stake out the shop. Then you can follow him in and start up a conversation."

When he leads me through town to a restaurant, I'm surprised. "Is this where they sell the clocks?"

"No, that's across the street. See it over there? I

thought we'd wait here until Hamish shows. Hungry?"

"Not really. But I guess I could have some coffee while we wait."

"You'll need more than coffee," he says to me. Then he speaks in rapid-fire German to the server and orders for me.

"I said I wasn't hungry."

"You can't visit Rudesheim and not try the leberknödel."

"Please tell me it's not made with stomach parts," I say. "Once was enough for me."

"No stomach," Erich says. "I promise you'll love the leberknödel. I order it every time I'm in Rudesheim."

"What is lubberknuckle?"

When I stumble over the German pronunciation, Erich smiles. "Leberknödel," he repeats slowly. "Knödel means dumpling."

"Oh, I love dumplings," I say.

The waiter deposits two steins of beer on the table, and Erich makes a toast. "Here's to an efficient partnership."

"An *efficient* partnership?" This must be business-like Erich's new take on team building. Beer instead of champagne. I take a sip of my beer, then add, "You Germans do love efficiency, don't you? What is it they say about Germany—the trains always run on time?"

"I can assure you that the trains do not always run on time," Erich says. "Just last week, my train was twenty seconds behind schedule."

"Was that a joke? No, I take that back. You're not the joking type."

"That's not true. I have a sense of humor." Erich says something in German, then chuckles. When I stare at him pointedly, he translates, "Can a kangaroo jump higher than a house? Yes, because a house can't jump."

I roll my eyes. "Like I said, you're not the joking type."

"Ah, here it is." Erich motions for the waiter to set a plate in front of me. "Your leberknödel."

"It looks good." I take a cautious bite of the dumpling, then nod approvingly. "It's tasty. What did you get?"

"Blutwurst." Erich slices off a piece of sausage and spreads coarse mustard on it before popping it into his mouth.

After taking a bite of sauerkraut and mashed potatoes, I ask, "Is that like bratwurst?"

"Kind of, except it's made with blood."

I shudder. "Gross. I'd never eat that, or anything made with organ meats."

"Organ meats?"

"Yeah, you know, like heart, kidney, liver," I say. "My mom used to make liver and onions every Thursday night. It was revolting, so one week my sister and I went on a hunger strike and refused to eat it. She tried to serve it to us again for breakfast the next day. But turns out we could out-stubborn my mother, so it went off the menu."

Erich points at my plate. "So, you like the leberknödel?"

"So good." I devour the rest of the dumplings, then dab my napkin to my lips. "I'd definitely order them again. How do you pronounce it again?"

"Leberknödel."

"You said that 'knödel' means dumplings, right?" After Erich nods, I ask, "So what does 'leber' mean?"

"Promise you won't get mad." Erich bites back a smile. "It means liver."

My eyes widen, and I make a choking sound. "Liver? I ate liver dumplings?"

"Yes, and you enjoyed them."

I gulp down my beer to wash the taste of liver out of my mouth. "No more ordering for me. Understood?"

Erich points at his plate. "Want to try some of my blutwurst?"

"No, I do not want to eat your blood sausage. Next thing I know you're going to tell me that the mashed potatoes were made with marshmallows."

"No, I would never do that to anyone. Marshmallows are horrible."

"Well, at least there's one thing we can agree on." I take another sip of beer, then say, "You said that you order leberknödel whenever you're in Rudesheim. Is this where you were raised?"

Erich averts his eyes and fiddles with his silverware. "Um—"

An oompah band marches down the street, and the sound of the tuba drowns Erich out. I'm fascinated by the lederhosen that the men wear. When they finally depart, the waiter asks Erich something in German.

I hold my hand up, "Do not let him order dessert for me."

The waiter laughs, then says in English, "No, I was asking your boyfriend if you wanted any coffee."

I feel my face grow warm. "My boyfriend?"

Erich folds his arms across his chest and shakes his head. "She is not my girlfriend."

"And he is not my boyfriend," I say.

"Sorry. It seemed like you were a couple," the waiter says apologetically. "Would either of you like dessert? Coffee?"

"We would like some . . ." Erich's voice trails off when I glare at him. "Sorry, you go ahead and order for yourself."

"I'd like some strudel, please."

"Make that two," Erich says.

After the waiter departs, I say, "I can't believe he thought we were a couple."

"Yes, it's obvious that we don't have feelings for each other," Erich says.

"True, the only feelings I have for you are as a partner. An efficient partner."

Erich looks across the street, then says, "I don't

think you'll have time to have your strudel. Hamish just went into the cuckoo clock shop."

* * *

"Can you get my strudel to go?" I yell over my shoulder as I dash toward the cuckoo clock shop. Then I halt in my tracks, spin around and say, "Make sure it's made with apples, not liver."

Erich nods, but I'm not quite sure I believe him. He'll probably tell the waiter to make my strudel with a variety of organ meats. If you can't trust a guy to order food for you, can you really trust him with anything?

General Taylor did vouch for him, though. So I'm sure Erich's good at what he does. He can be trusted with spy stuff, but nothing else. Not my food, not my heart, not my—

I slam the door firmly on that train of thought and enter the shop. The sound of cuckoos signaling that it's two o'clock greets me. If you've never been in a room full of hundreds of cuckoo clocks all going off at the same time, I don't recommend it unless you have earplugs.

Okay, let see. The cuckoos are telling me that it's two. That means I have an hour before I'm supposed to escort the passengers back to the boat. That gives me about forty-five minutes before I have to leave the shop and get to the meeting point on time. Can I engage Hamish in conversation and bond with him over Scrabble by then? I really don't have a choice. We'll be in Amsterdam in less than a week, and if Hamish doesn't ask me to be on his Scrabble team, the mission is toast.

Before I even open my mouth, the shop owner greets me in English and asks me what state I'm from. Why is it that Europeans can tell an American from a mile away? After telling him that I'm from the great state of Texas, I wander through a series of small, interconnected rooms, each one full of clocks. I can see why a collector like Hamish would come here.

I'm starting to wonder if Hamish has sneaked out the back door when I spot him inspecting a display of jewelry in a glass case. Each piece features cuckoo clocks, and some of them even look like they're functional. Hamish seems drawn to a charm bracelet. This is the perfect opening. I extend my arm so that my Scrabble charm bracelet is on full display, point at the one he's examining and say, "That's gorgeous."

Oblivious to my jewelry, he says absentmindedly, "When I was younger, I used to have a girlfriend who loved charm bracelets. She was a fine lassie."

"What happened to her?"

Hamish strokes his beard and stares off into the distance. "I did something I knew she wouldn't approve of, so I broke up with her. She ended up marrying another man. Lucky bloke."

"I'm sorry," I say, still waving my charm bracelet

around like a madwoman.

"She's a widow now." Hamish gives a heavy sigh.

"Maybe the two of you can get back together. You always hear about second-chance romances. Couples who broke up only to get back together later in life."

"No, you can't go back in time," he says decisively. "I've learned that the hard way."

Noticing that Hamish's cane is propped up against the display cabinet, I pick it up. "This is stunning." I run my fingers along the wood, making note of the faint groove by the handle. "My grandfather would love one of these. Where did you get it?"

Hamish's face darkens. "It's a one-of-a-kind."

He goes to grab the cane from me and stumbles. I steady him and help him sit on a nearby chair. "Are you okay?"

He grips his cane tightly in his hands, then his gaze drifts to my wrist. "Are those Scrabble tiles?"

I resist the urge to do a fist pump in the air. "They are. I got this bracelet when I won the Nationals."

"You're a Scrabble champion?" Hamish asks.

"Uh-huh. Do you play?"

"I dabble in the game," he says, downplaying his abilities.

I smile brightly at Hamish. "It's been so long since I've played. Would you be interested in a match tonight after dinner?"

Hamish gets to his feet. "I'd be delighted to, young lady."

After we make arrangements to meet later, Hamish excuses himself to go talk about winding mechanisms with the shop owner.

I make my way back to the restaurant and give Erich a big thumbs up.

* * *

I wake up the next morning with a spring in my step, still riding on the high of winning three games of Scrabble in a row last night.

After a three-year hiatus from the word game, it felt so good to play again. The excitement of drawing for first play, the feel of the wooden tiles against my fingers, the thrill of placing 'Q' on the triple-letter score square, and the rush when I played all of my seven tiles in a single turn. I was in heaven.

Hamish looked at me appreciatively when I won our final game with 'zaxes.' And I have to confess, I might have even gloated a little. I'm counting the hours until our rematch tonight. It's going to be hard to concentrate on my tour manager duties today because all my brain wants to focus on are obscure two and three-letter words.

I practically skip to breakfast—skip is worth ten points, by the way—and greet Auguste Renoir cheerfully when I enter the kitchen.

"Silence. Auguste Renoir does not like to be disturbed when he is making omelets." The chef lobs an egg at me and it narrowly misses me. "Out of his kitchen."

"Hey, you could have hurt me," I say.

"That was the idea," he snarls. "Clean that mess up, then get out."

"Mind if I grab a piece of toast first?" I ask tentatively.

"Out!"

As I run out of the kitchen, I hear several eggs splatter against the wall.

I walk through the dining room, saying good morning to everyone. I suggest that they may want to consider something other than omelets. "I think the chef might be short of eggs," I explain. "Perhaps some toast and bacon instead?"

Emma and Hank are seated at a table by the window, and they motion me over. "There's our fellow southerner," Emma says. "We haven't seen you since yesterday morning."

After chatting about our favorite southern dishes, I ask them how their excursion yesterday was. "You went on the wine tasting tour, right?"

Hank grins. "Emma got a little tipsy."

Emma bats her husband's hand and says, "They shouldn't give you all that free wine if they don't expect you to drink it. Have you tried the local riesling yet, dear?"

"I tried some in Mainz, but not in Rudesheim," I say. "But I did have a nice beer yesterday."

"Oh, you should have had a glass. I liked the sweet ones. Hank liked his 'trocken.' That means 'dry' in German.

"You certainly seemed to have learned a lot about wine."

"She was the teacher's pet." Hank beams at his wife. "Of course, it comes naturally to her, seeing as she was an elementary teacher before she retired."

"What grade did you teach?" I ask.

"Second," she said. "Such a sweet age."

I turn to Hank. "What line of work were you in?"

"I had a security firm," he says.

"Oh, like bodyguards?"

Hank shakes his head. "No, more along the lines of securing company property during transport. Making sure it gets from one destination to another."

"That sounds interesting." I stand and excuse myself. "I have to get going. See you later for the excursion to the Ehrenbreitstein Fortress?"

"Yes, dear, see you then," Emma says.

Rather than risk running into Frau Albrecht in the reception area, I exit onto the deck and take the back stairs down to the crew quarters. Whistling the theme song from *Jeopardy*, I open the door to my cabin. When I see Erich sitting on my bunk eating a piece of toast, my good mood evaporates.

I don't even bother to ask how he got into my cabin. I just hope that Sophia or any of the other crewmembers didn't see him. There are already enough rumors floating around this ship about my supposed affair with Erich.

"Your breakfast is over there. There's black coffee and I took the liberty of ordering you dry toast. That way, you'll know that there's nothing in your breakfast but bread. No kidney, liver or the like. Scout's honor."

"You're German. What do you know about the Boy Scouts?"

"We have Boy Scouts in Germany. They're called . . ." Erich frowns, then says, "Never mind. Eat your breakfast quickly. We have work to do."

"We? I think you mean I have work to do," I say. "In forty-five minutes, I'm leading an excursion. Will you be joining? Or are you going to stay here?" I ask sarcastically.

"I think I'll stay here," he says. "I have an activity planned."

"What? Lying on a lounge chair on the sun deck?"

"No, more of an exploratory activity."

"Exploratory . . . oh, my gosh. You're going to break into Hamish's room, aren't you?"

Erich holds up a card key. "Is it really 'breaking in' if you have a master key? Now, I need you to text me once the group is at Ehrenbreitstein Fortress and confirm that Hamish is with you. Can you do that?"

"I think I know how to text," I say in between bites of dry toast.

"You're missing something critical."

"Yeah, I know. Butter."

"No, if you're going to text me you need . . ." He pauses as though we're in a game show.

I channel my inner *Jeopardy* contestant. "What's a phone? Don't worry, it's in my purse." I take a sip of black coffee and wince. There's a reason why cows were created, namely for their cream.

"You need my number." Erich reaches into my purse and pulls out my phone. This man has no sense of privacy. He types in his phone number, somehow managing to circumvent my password protection. "While I'm here, I'm going to clear your search history."

"Uh, no you're not."

"Yes, I am. What do you think would happen if your phone fell into the wrong hands? What would people think if they saw your search history?"

"It's not like I'm looking at porn sites," I say. "Just some shopping sites and social media."

"Oh, Isabelle, do you think I'm stupid? You've been doing searches on how to be a spy. It sent off alarm bells at headquarters. If you want to know how to be a spy, all you have to do is ask. I'll be happy to teach you."

Erich clicks a few buttons, then hands my phone back to me. "Are you going to finish that?" he asks, pointing at the lone piece of toast on the plate.

"No, take it. Without butter, it tastes like cardboard."

He leaves my cabin, munching on his dry toast, and I sink onto my bed. If Erich knows what I'm searching for on the Internet, does he know about the texts to my friends? The texts where I talk about the mysterious hot guy I met?

CHAPTER 7
WEREWOLF SIDE EFFECTS

Later that night, Hamish and I have a Scrabble rematch in the lounge. I feel nervous, not because of the large crowd that has gathered around to watch, but because of Erich. He's sitting at the bar, sipping on scotch, looking at me. Not at the Scrabble board like everyone else, but directly at me.

Is he trying to communicate something telepathically to me? If so, what? An update on what he found when he searched Hamish's room earlier today? A word that I can make with a "Q," but no "U"? How he really feels about me?

Ignoring Erich's uncomfortable stare, I lay down my tiles. One of the people watching says, "Qapik? That's not a real word."

"It sure is a real word. It's Azerbaijanian money,"

Hank tells the man. Then he pats me on the shoulder. "Well played, Isabelle."

Hamish ignores the chatter and inspects the tiles on his rack. When a smile creeps across his face, I steel myself. He's a worthy opponent. His ability to recognize word-building opportunities is impressive. This is one of those times, and I groan as he builds off my "Q" to spell "quixotic."

Quixotic—the unrealistic and impractical pursuit of something. That's what this mission feels like to me. Erich is hoping for the impossible from me, that I'll be able to stop Hamish from selling the stolen emerald to the bad guys. His faith in my abilities is idealistic at best. Foolish at worst.

I can't believe I let General Taylor talk me into helping Erich. The general pushed all of my buttons, appealing to my sense of duty and desire to stop the unthinkable from happening. But his faith in me is misplaced. Not too long ago, I was working at a mini-mart.

Hamish interrupts my thoughts, laying down the rest of his tiles. "I think I won this one, lassie."

After we total up our points, I concede the game.

"Should we go again?" he asks.

I waver. "I'm not sure. It's getting late. Maybe we should call it a night."

Hank leans forward. "You gotta play one more game, sweetheart. I've got money riding on you."

I turn to look at him. "You're betting on Scrabble?"

"Sure thing." He grins. "It's like betting on *Jeopardy*. Even if you lose your shirt, you feel smart doing it."

Emma confides, "I could never get Hank to sit still long enough to play Scrabble. It's a real treat to see him so interested in it."

I nod at Hamish. "Okay, one more game."

"You won't regret it, lassie. Well, that is unless you lose again." Hamish winks at me, then suggests we take a fifteen-minute break first. While he goes off to the restroom, Max approaches the table.

"I'd like to get some pictures of you playing Scrabble," he says. "Zoe thinks it might be a nice addition to the article. Two champions playing each other on a riverboat is a unique angle."

"Okay," I say. "Hamish will be back soon."

"In the meantime, let's take some pictures of just you posing with the Scrabble board." Max shows me where he wants me to sit, then touches the side of my head. "How about if you take your hair down?"

"Oh, I can't. If you have long hair, you're required to wear it in a tight bun."

Max makes a show of looking around the lounge. "I don't think anyone here is going to rat you out."

The hairpins are pressing painfully on my scalp, so I let Max convince me. After I pull my hair loose, I run my fingers through it to untangle it.

"So much better," Max says appreciatively. Then he pushes a lock of my hair behind my ear.

"Gorgeous."

"Thinking of becoming a hair stylist?" Zoe has her hands on her hips and she's glaring at her colleague. "Because if you're looking for a career change, I'd be more than happy to call our manager and tell her to send another photographer out to replace you."

"She's just jealous," Max says in a stage whisper.

"Photographs," Zoe snarls. "Any day now."

"Someone's touchy." Max grins at Zoe, but gets to work, taking several photos of me from various angles.

When Hamish returns to the table, he politely refuses to have his picture taken. "No thanks, young man. This ugly face might break your camera. Focus on the bonnie lass instead."

My phone beeps. It's a text from Erich: *More focus on the mission. Less focus on flirting.*

Oh, boy, he hasn't seen flirting yet. I slip my hand through Max's arm. "Can I see the pictures you took?"

While Max shows them to me, I make sure to lean in closer. I glance back at Erich, curious to see his reaction. But all I see is a vacant barstool and an empty glass.

* * *

Erich avoided me for the rest of the night. The following day, I thought I might see him on the excursion to Cologne, but he didn't make an appearance. His loss, really, as the rest of the passengers had a great time. I think I'm getting the hang of being a tour manager. The key is to make sure you know where the restrooms are located—that's the number one question I get from the passengers—and keep everyone hydrated in the warm summer weather.

"Wasn't the Chocolate Museum amazing?" Zoe asks me.

We're sitting on the sun deck, enjoying an after-dinner drink while the boat makes its way from Cologne to the Netherlands.

"I noticed Max got you some hazelnut pralines," I say to her.

"Oh, he didn't buy them for me," Zoe says. "He tried to give them to that Australian girl, but when she told him she had a boyfriend back in Sydney, he handed them to me. Like some sort of consolation prize."

I cock my head to one side. "I'm not so sure that's what was going on. I think he did that to make you jealous. He always intended to give you those chocolates."

"I've worked with Max for years. If he liked me romantically, I'd know by now. All we do is fight like cats and dogs." Zoe gives me a sideways look. "If anyone's jealous, it's Erich. Every time he sees Max talking to you, he's got daggers in his eyes."

I sit up straight. "Do you really think he's jealous?"

Zoe grins. "You like Erich, don't you?"

"No, of course not. Besides, the crew aren't allowed to become romantically involved with the passengers."

"Yeah, that's what's holding you back," she says dryly.

"Even if I liked him," I hold up my hand, "and that's a big 'if,' I still wouldn't want to get involved with him."

"Why? Because he'll be getting off the boat once we get to Amsterdam?" Zoe asks.

Oh, wow, once the mission is over, I'll never see Erich again. I chew on my lip as that sinks in.

"Earth to Isabelle," Zoe says. "That's what it is, isn't it? You don't want to lose your heart to someone you won't see again."

I take a deep breath, then let it out slowly. "I guess so."

"Hah, you admitted it," Zoe says triumphantly. "You're sweet on him."

I smile. "My friends would say that I'm smitten with him."

"Smitten. That's cute," Zoe says. "I love old-fashioned sayings like that. Isabelle is smitten with Erich," she says in a sing-songy voice. "First comes love, then comes marriage, then comes Isabelle pushing the baby carriage."

I laugh despite myself. "Erich is the last person who would ever settle down and get married, let alone have kids. It wouldn't be possible in his line of work."

"What does he do?" Zoe asks.

"Uh, he's a pharmaceutical sales representative."

"That doesn't seem like the type of career that's incompatible with getting married and starting a family," Zoe points out.

I try to come up with a plausible rationale for Erich remaining single. "I think the drugs he sells have some serious side-effects."

"Like infertility? There's always adoption."

"No, it's not that he can't have children," I say. "The drugs cause hair to grow out of inappropriate places."

"You realize that happens to everyone as they get older." Zoe taps the space between her upper lip and her nose. "Women grow mustaches and men have hair coming out of their ears."

"No, I'm talking about hair in thick patches all over his body. Fur, really." I realize I'm digging myself in further, so I go for broke. "Like a werewolf. He has to shave ten times a day."

"You're making that up," Zoe says.

I shrug. "This is silly. I met Erich a few days ago. It's not like I'm even thinking about a serious relationship with him. But . . ."

"But you are thinking about something with him." Zoe gives me a sympathetic look. "Maybe you should let that something happen and see what it leads to."

"Well, nothing is going to happen if he thinks Max is interested in me."

Zoe cocks her head to one side. "Really? Most guys like that sort of challenge."

"I can't see Erich fighting for me."

"Okay, I have a crazy idea," Zoe says. "What if I make it seem like Max and I are a couple? Then Erich would think that he has a clear field."

"How would you do that?"

Zoe stares off into space for a moment, then looks back at me. "I could kiss him," she says shyly. "All you have to do is arrange for Erich to see me plant one on Max."

"Really? You want to kiss your arch-enemy?"

"We ladies have to stick together," she jokes. "Besides, it's for a good cause."

"I'm not sure this is a smart idea."

"Because he's a passenger?"

"Right now my manager suspects I'm having an affair with Erich, but if she ever had proof that I actually was having inappropriate relations with him, she'd fire me and I'd end up back at the mini-mart."

Zoe interrupts my thoughts. "I can't picture you working at a mini-mart."

"Yeah, me neither," I say wryly. "It was meant to be a temporary gig, but ended up lasting for three years. Thankfully, my friend Mia convinced me to come to Europe with her. We were about to book airplane tickets when I won a free cruise for the two of us from the States to Europe. It seemed like a sign. Then I saw an advertisement for this job, and the rest is history."

"Yay for Mia," Zoe says. Then she grabs my hand. "Hey, there's Max. Why don't you go track down Erich and lure him up here? Give me a sign and then I'll fake kiss Max."

* * *

Somehow Zoe has convinced me this is a good idea. I find Erich sitting in the lounge, leafing through a magazine. "How come you're not playing Scrabble with Hamish?" he asks.

"He wanted a night off. Said the arthritis in his knee is acting up." I furrow my brow. "Although I'm not sure how you can be a jewel thief if you need a cane to walk."

"Or things aren't what they appear to be."

"Are you saying that he's faking it?" When Erich shrugs, I jab a finger in his direction. "Oh, come on. You'd know if he's faking it. You have a file on him."

"I'm not in the mood to play games with you tonight," Erich says. "Why don't you go find your boyfriend, Max? I'm sure he'd be happy to entertain you."

"He's not my boyfriend, and don't you go starting that rumor. His girlfriend would be livid if you did."

"What girlfriend?"

"Zoe."

"The two of them are a couple?" Erich looks puzzled. "But then why does he keep flirting with you?"

"They had a fight. I think he was trying to make Zoe jealous." I take the magazine from Erich and close it. "I need to talk with you about something."

"We can talk here," he says.

"No, someplace more private. Let's go up to the sun deck."

When we walk out on deck, I see Max and Zoe standing at the railing. Max's back is to me, so I give Zoe a covert signal.

Zoe grabs Max's hand, then pulls him toward her. As she kisses him, I nudge Erich. "See, they're a couple."

Erich looks at them, then gives me an appraising look. "It's funny, but sometimes the people you least expect to get together do."

Wow, those two are getting pretty passionate. For a fake kiss, there sure are some sparks. I give Zoe a covert thumbs up, then clear my throat. "Maybe we should go someplace else," I suggest to Erich.

Erich nods. "We'll go to my stateroom."

He heads down the stairs, and I hurry to catch up with him. "I don't think that's a good idea."

"You were the one who wanted to talk with me privately."

"Yeah, but Frau Albrecht saw me in your room the other night. What will she think if I'm seen there a second time?"

"It doesn't matter what she thinks," Erich says as we walk down the corridor. "What matters is what the passengers think, and they're singing your praises."

When we reach his cabin, I double check to make sure no one is watching before I slip inside. He motions for me to sit, then continues. "You're a natural problem-solver and you think quickly on your feet. You were wasted working in that mini-mart."

"I'm coming to realize that too," I say. "My contract on the riverboat runs until November. So I guess I have between now and then to figure out what I want to do."

"Why not go back into intelligence? General Taylor won't say what happened to you in the Air Force and why you left. But I do know the issue is about confidence, not ability."

"Stop pretending you don't know," I snap. "I'm sure it's in my file."

"Not the copy I have." Erich runs his fingers through his hair. "You probably don't believe me though."

I chew on my lip. "It doesn't matter. It's in the past."

"Well, if you ever want to talk about it, I'm here for you," he says earnestly.

"Thanks," I say. "Listen, I'm beat. I'm going to head off."

As I walk toward the door, Erich asks, "Wait, before you go, what is it you wanted to talk with me about?"

"Oh, um . . . if anyone asks, you're a pharmaceutical sales representative."

"I am?"

"Yeah, that's the cover story I gave Zoe and Sophia."

"Look at you, creating cover stories for me," he says, smiling despite himself.

"And another thing, the reason you're single is because the drugs you sell have side-effects."

"Really? What kind of side effects?"

"Let's just say you're very hairy underneath those clothes. Like werewolf-hairy."

"So you think about what I look like without my clothes on?"

My face grows warm and I stare down at the carpet. "No, I don't have to think about it. I saw you in a towel the other day."

"And I resembled a werewolf?"

"No, not at all. I just panicked when I was talking with Zoe about you and that's what I came up with."

"So exactly why were you talking about my relationship status with Zoe, anyway?"

I rub my temples. This is not my best conversational moment. Fearing what the next words out of my mouth might be, I yank Erich's door open. "Is that the fire alarm? I better go investigate." Then I rush down the corridor, praying that he doesn't come after me.

CHAPTER 8
IS NORMAL OVERRATED?

No, there wasn't a fire. Erich knew that, but he let me go. Upon reflection, I realized that General Taylor probably didn't share the details of what happened in the Air Force—he had agreed to keep what happened between the two of us. Erich had been genuinely concerned and was sincere in offering to listen if I wanted to talk. Is it possible for a guy to be secretive and not be a jerk? I'm beginning to think it might just be.

I slept fitfully last night, haunted by strange dreams of Erich turning into a werewolf. So when I board the tour bus that will take us to the Rijksmuseum in Amsterdam, I'm carrying an extra large coffee with lots of cream and sugar.

I finish caffeinating my system when the bus pulls

up in front of the museum. After tossing my cup in the trashcan, I hold an umbrella over my head. "Alright, everyone, this way to see masterpieces by the Dutch masters, Rembrandt and Vermeer."

As I lead the group into the atrium, Erich suddenly appears. "I didn't see you on the bus," I say, trying to adopt a casual tone.

"I had an early meeting in Amsterdam," he says. "So I took a taxi here."

The sunlight flooding through the glass roof illuminates dark circles under Erich's eyes, circles I haven't seen before. "Is everything okay?"

"Of course," he says. "We're on track for the mission."

"No, I meant you. Are you okay?"

Erich points at a man holding a clipboard. "I think that's your tour guide."

As I walk over to introduce myself, I wonder why Erich is avoiding my question. I chat for a few moments with the tour guide, then he introduces himself to the group. After an overview of the Rijksmuseum, we head to the Gallery of Honour where some of the most famous works are housed. When we pause in front of *A Mother's Duty* by Pieter de Hooch, the group laughs when the guide explains it depicts a woman delousing her child.

The tone becomes more serious when we view Rembrandt's *The Jewish Bride*. "Some people believe this painting depicts Isaac and Rebecca disguising themselves as brother and sister so that they could escape King Abimelech," the guide explains. "However, see how Isaac has his arm around Rebecca? Unable to hide their love for each other, they are sharing a tender moment."

"Aw, isn't that sweet," Emma says to her husband.

Hank puts his arm around Emma, unconsciously mimicking the pose from the painting. "Sure is. You can't hide what you feel for someone."

Erich and my eyes meet and we hold each other's gaze for a very long moment, almost as though we're playing chicken. I lose, but only because someone jostles me.

As the group traipses to the next alcove in the gallery, Erich lingers, looking at *The Jewish Bride.*

"There's something wrong," I say to him. "What is it?"

He shakes his head. "I don't want to worry you."

"Well, I'm already worried, so you might as well spill the beans."

Erich paces back and forth for a moment, then says, "Headquarters hasn't been able to eliminate Hamish's partner for the Scrabble tournament."

I wring my hands. "Please tell me you don't mean what I think you mean when you say 'eliminate.'"

"What?" Erich takes a step back. "No. Poor choice of words. He's not going to be harmed."

"That's a relief." I glance over at the tour group to make sure they haven't moved on. "What happens if you can't 'eliminate' him, so to speak?"

"It *will* happen," Erich says. "I just thought it would have happened by now. Carry on as normal with Hamish, playing Scrabble."

"But the tournament is tomorrow," I point out.

"I'm well aware of that, Isabelle," he says sharply.

I clutch my stomach as waves of anxiety roll over me. Sitting on a nearby bench, I put my head in my hands.

Erich sits next to me and puts his arm around my shoulders. "Hey, I'm sorry. I didn't mean to snap at you."

"It's not that. It's the mission. I'm one of those people who compartmentalizes things. Always have. I put things into separate rooms in my brain, and that's how I stay in control. Except sometimes, those things escape from their separate rooms and collide in my brain. And then I panic."

Erich squeezes me tightly without saying a word. His quiet strength makes me feel safe.

"I'm a liability to this mission. There has to be some other way to shadow Hamish at the Scrabble tournament."

"I'm sorry," Erich says softly. "If there was another way, we would have done it. You're our only hope."

I twist my grandmother's ring around my finger, then take a deep breath. "It's fine. I can do it. Just promise me that after the tournament is over, my job is finished and I can go back to my normal life."

Erich nods. "I promise. Your life will go back to normal by the time tomorrow night rolls around."

Okay, that's settled, but I'm left with one nagging question—is a normal life what I want?

* * *

"Do you mind if we play in the library tonight instead of in the lounge?" Hamish asks me.

Hamish looks tired tonight. The way he's leaning so heavily on his cane, I wonder if he should be on his feet at all.

"Of course not."

"Thanks," he says as we walk slowly toward the library. "Do you ever have those days when you crave peace and quiet? On larger cruise ships, you can lose yourself in a crowd. But here on a riverboat when there's only two hundred passengers, it's hard to escape. Getting a cup of coffee takes at least a half hour because everyone knows you and wants to chat."

I hold open the door for him. "You sound like an introvert."

"Aye, lassie. I do need my alone time."

I hesitate before setting the Scrabble board on the table. "We don't have to play tonight."

"Ach, no, being with you is like being by myself, but better." He slowly sits in one of the armchairs. "You're a solace to my soul."

Hamish draws the low tile, so he gets to go first. He

places his first word—snath.

As he marks down his score, I ask, "The handle of a scythe?"

"That's correct. We Scrabble players are word freaks, aren't we? Our vocabulary is odd, to say the least."

I study the tiles on my rack. If I played off Hamish's "S," I could spell out "secret." It seems like a sign from the universe. Everyone has secrets—Hamish, Erich, and me. Flustered, I end up playing "set," earning myself a whopping three points in the process.

"That the best you can do, lassie?" Hamish asks. "You seem distracted tonight. Boyfriend troubles?"

I snort. "I don't have a boyfriend."

"What about that good-looking man I saw you talking to the other night?"

"I talk to all the men, good-looking or not. It's part of my job."

"No, this was different. There was definitely chemistry between the two of you."

I frown. Has everyone seen the sparks between Erich and me? Trying to misdirect him, I say, "I'm not sure who you mean."

"That German fellow."

"There are several Germans on the cruise." I point at the board. "It's your turn."

"Point taken. I shouldn't butt into your love life." Hamish strokes his beard. "Remember that woman I told you about in the cuckoo clock shop?"

"The one that got away?"

"That's the one. She was always interfering in other people's love lives. She enjoyed nothing more than to set people up. Or better, helping get them back together if they had broken up." Hamish's smile fades and he goes back to studying his tiles.

"What are your plans after you disembark tomorrow?" I ask, trying to lighten the mood. "Are you going to spend some time in Amsterdam?"

"Oh, I thought you knew. I'm playing in the second annual European Scrabble team tournament this weekend."

"I have to confess, it seems odd to play Scrabble as part of a team," I say. "That's more common for school tournaments, isn't it?"

Hamish nods. "It is an unusual format. But it's a lot of fun. My partner and I complement each other."

I glance at the clock. It's already ten, and Hamish is still talking about playing with his partner. It doesn't look like headquarters has managed to "eliminate" Hamish's teammate. The mission has already failed before it began properly.

We continue to play, and I resign myself to spending tomorrow here on the riverboat, not at a Scrabble tournament helping to stop an international arms deal. Just when I'm about to excuse myself for the night, Sophia enters the room.

She hands Hamish a folded piece of paper. "I have

a message for you, Mr. MacDougall."

Hamish reads it, then groans.

"Bad news?"

"Yes, my partner is stuck in Istanbul. He won't be back in time for the tournament tomorrow." Hamish folds the note and sticks it in his pocket. "Funny. I didn't even know he was going to Turkey."

"Oh, that's too bad. I know how much you were looking forward to playing Scrabble with him."

Hamish gives me a considered look. "You wouldn't want to . . ." He shakes his head. "No, I shouldn't ask."

"Ask what?"

"Would you consider playing in the tournament with me tomorrow? You'd be doing me a real favor."

"Actually, I'd love to," I say with a huge grin on my face.

Hamish grins back. "What are the odds my partner would have to withdraw at the last minute and I happen to make the acquaintance of a Scrabble champion on this cruise?"

"It's quite the coincidence." That's what I say, but we all know I don't believe that. If a covert organization is pulling the strings, then it's amazing how dramatically your odds increase.

* * *

I text Erich the good news and he tells me to meet him on the sun deck. When I come up the stairs, I'm relieved to see that he's the only one up there. He rushes toward me and scoops me up in his arms. With his hands cinched around my waist, he twirls us around. "You did it, Isabelle. You got him to ask you to be his Scrabble partner," he says in my ear. "You're incredible."

With each spin, he presses my body tighter against his. His muscles are taut. His breath is hot against my skin. His lips whisper my name.

I wrap my hands around his neck and brush my cheek against his. He trembles and just when I think he's going to kiss me, he abruptly sets me down.

"Sorry, I got carried away," he says.

"Yeah, I think you might have let your self-control slip a bit there." I try to say it with a light, teasing tone, but my voice cracks as I wrestle with my own self-control.

"Are you okay?" Erich starts to reach for me, but stops himself and shoves his hands in his pockets. "You seem a little . . . um, tense."

"Tense? Me? You're the one whose eyes are dilated," I say.

"Of course, they're dilated. It's nighttime."

"Oh, is that the reason why?"

Erich takes a step back, re-establishing a respectable amount of space between us. "Your eyes dilate to let in more light. It's a scientific fact," he says.

His self-discipline is back. I hate it. Something

needs to be done about it. I want to kiss him until he loses control.

"Isabelle, what are you doing?" Erich asks as I close the gap between us.

I run my hands up his arms, my fingers tracing his biceps before resting on his broad shoulders. "I think I liked you better when you got carried away."

Erich's breathing becomes shallow. "We can't get carried away."

I nibble on his earlobe. "Speak for yourself."

"*I* can't get carried away," Erich says. His voice is husky. His control is slipping.

"Why?" I stroke Erich's neck with my fingernails.

"The mission . . ." His voice trails off as he places his hands on the small of my back.

I turn my head so that my lips hover a fraction from his. "Do you want me to kiss you, Erich? Or do you want to talk about the mission?"

He doesn't use words to answer me. He uses his mouth, pressing his lips against mine. Our first kiss is tentative, but any gentleness quickly dissipates. We can't get enough of each other.

My head is spinning, my heart is pounding, my skin feels flushed. I don't know what self-control is anymore. This goes on for an eternity. Then a tiny voice in my head makes itself known.

Remember what happened in the Air Force, Isabelle.

And just like that, my self-control is back. I push Erich away, take a deep breath, then say coolly,

"You're right, Erich. We can't do this. The mission comes first."

CHAPTER 9
THE DOG ATE MY HOMEWORK

Frau Albrecht frowns when I walk into the reception area the next morning. "That outfit is unacceptable. Where's your uniform?"

Personally, I think my outfit is totally acceptable. Say goodbye to that ill-fitting suit and scratchy polyester blouse. The floaty sundress and sandals I have on are far more my style. And wearing my hair loose over my shoulders is such a relief after having it pinned back in that awful bun.

Sophia looks up from the computer and her face lights up. "Does this mean you're quitting?"

"No, I just have the day off," I say.

"The day off? Are you kidding me? You only started working here a week ago. I haven't had a day off in three months." Sophia turns to Frau Albrecht.

"How come she gets time off and I don't?"

"Isabelle most certainly does not have the day off." Frau Albrecht taps her pen on the counter. "Unless you are planning on resigning, then we need you here at the front desk. The current passengers are disembarking, and then we have a four-hour window to get the boat ready for the next set of passengers. Now go back to your cabin and change into your uniform. The alternative is handing in your letter of resignation."

"But, um . . ."

"Um, what?" the older woman says.

Last night Erich had promised that he would arrange for me to have the day off so I can play in the Scrabble tournament. Did he finally find some strings he couldn't pull?

"Well?" Frau Albrecht asks impatiently. Then her phone rings. She grunts hello, listens for a few moments while cracking her knuckles. Then she gives me a full on glare. "Apparently, Isabelle does have the day off."

Sophia looks like she wants to roast me on a spit.

"I'll be back this evening," I say, rushing to get off the boat before Sophia hurls a stapler at me.

When I walk onto the dock, Erich is leaning against a car.

I'm not sure what to say to him or what to do. After what happened last night, I foolishly hoped we'd be able to avoid each other. But we have a mission to do. Together.

Erich is wearing his game face. Just another day at the office for him. When I ended the kiss last night, he looked stunned, but only for an instant. He quickly regained his composure and agreed that getting involved romantically was a bad idea.

"Hi," I say. "I didn't expect to see you today."

"Really? I told you I'd drive you to the tournament." He opens the passenger door. "Hop in."

I slip into the car, clutching my purse on my lap. We drive to the venue in an uncomfortable silence. To pass the time, I review the tournament rules.

Unlike the tournaments I've played in before, where one player is pitted against another player, this is a tag-team event. Each team has two people. Each player in a team has their own rack of tiles, one playing right after the other one before the next team takes over. This works out great for me. Because Hamish will be sitting next to me the entire tournament, I can keep a close eye on him.

Teams are seeded according to their ratings from their players' associations. Hamish and his former partner were the number two seed. But because I haven't played Scrabble competitively in several years, and don't have a current rating, Hamish has gone in early to the tournament to discuss the situation with the officials. Part of me feels guilty that, because Hamish's partner was "eliminated" and

I've taken his place, we may end up seeded near the bottom. It would be an embarrassing ranking for someone of Hamish's caliber.

"We're here," Erich says, as he pulls up in front of a hotel in the heart of Amsterdam. He puts the car in park. "Let's go over the plan one more time."

His tone is businesslike. I shift my body to face him and adopt a neutral expression. "Go ahead."

"Stick close to Hamish. According to our intel, he's supposed to make the exchange with the fence during the tournament."

"How's he going to do it? It's not like you can casually hand over an emerald necklace."

"We don't know, and before you ask, we don't know what the fence looks like either. That's why you're there, to observe everything that's going on. Take pictures of everyone he talks to, everyone he looks at, everyone he nods to, everyone—"

"Yeah, I think I got it. Take pictures of everyone." I pull my phone out of my purse. "I better make sure this is fully charged. Yikes, it's down to twenty percent."

Erich reaches across me and opens the glove box. "Don't worry, I've got you covered. Use this one instead."

As he passes me a new phone, his fingers brush against the back of my hand. We both look at each other, conscious of the electricity between us.

I avert my eyes and rummage through my purse

again. "You know what? I think I have a charger in here somewhere. Yep, there it is." Holding his phone gingerly with the tips of my fingers so that we don't have to make contact, I try to give it back to him. "Here you go."

He shakes his head. "No, you have to use the phone I gave you. The photos you take will automatically upload to our servers. We'll be able to match them against our files so that we can identify the fence."

"Hmm . . . you've already been monitoring my phone—a total invasion of privacy which I'd like to mention again for the record—so I assumed you'd be able to see what photos I took on it already."

Avoiding my invasion of privacy point, he says, "This phone has certain special features that yours doesn't."

"Ooh, like a James Bond phone? Can it shoot bullets or bake bread?"

Erich gives me a slight smile. "Bake bread?"

"I missed breakfast," I say. "I was busy studying my Scrabble word lists. Anyway, what does it do?"

"See this red button on the side? Push that to zoom in when you're taking photos. And, if at any point you feel like you're in danger or you need urgent help, press the star button on the keypad."

I look at the phone incredulously. "That's it? Those are the special features? Don't you guys have your own Q? Even if this thing can't make sourdough bread, I expected something more impressive."

"You do realize that James Bond and Q are fictional characters, don't you? You need to take this seriously, Isabelle. If anything were to happen to you . . ." Erich grips the steering wheel and mutters something under his breath. Then he turns to me and says, "Back to the plan. Don't interfere with Hamish making the exchange. We want him to pass the necklace to the fence. Your job is to get the photos so that we can identify him or her. Then we'll take over from there. Your part of the mission will be over."

"Understood." I tuck the phone Erich gave me into my purse. "So I meet you after the tournament for a debrief?"

"Correct." He points at the passenger door. "You better get going. Hamish will be waiting for you."

I try to find something else we need to discuss, something we need to cover, just so that I can put off going into the tournament. The role I play in the mission sounds easy on the face of it, but what if things don't go to plan? Actually, if I'm being honest with myself, there's another reason I don't want to get out of the car, and that has to do with Erich. Spending time with him has been exhilarating. Yes, there was that amazing kiss, but it's more than that.

"You don't have much time," Erich reminds me.

I reluctantly step out of the car. As I watch Erich drive away, I fiddle with the Scrabble charms dangling from my wrist. I used to love this bracelet. Now it will just be a bittersweet reminder of falling for someone I could never be with.

* * *

When I walk into the hotel ballroom, memories of my competitive Scrabble-playing days flood back. A sign hanging from the ceiling reads: *Welcome to the Second Annual European Scrabble Team Tournament.* There are fifty small tables dotted around the room, each with a Scrabble board, and a timer. At the front, several people are clustered around a large whiteboard. One of them is brandishing a dictionary while the others are arguing about something. Scrabble players always find things to debate—should certain words be banned, should there be a penalty for challenging valid words, and whether boards with a built-in Lazy Susan are a sacrilege.

Hamish is sitting on a small couch next to a buffet table. As I walk over to join him, I snatch a cheese and ham pastry. "Good news, bad news," he says. "Which one do you want first?"

"Good news, I guess."

"We're still the number two seed," Hamish says as he brushes some lint off his shirt.

"That is good news," I say. "How did that happen?"

"The officials are taking your previous championship status into account, but . . ." Hamish pauses to take a sip of coffee.

"I guess this is where the bad news comes in?"

"It's a provisional ranking. They're going to assess you during the warm-up round," Hamish says. "Before the tournament kicks off, there's a round of regular Scrabble games—one person against one person. Basically, it's a way for everyone to loosen up. The officials want to see how you perform. If you do well, then we'll keep our number two seed position."

"So no pressure, then," I say.

"Scrabblers, can I have your attention, please?" One of the officials calls the room to order. "My colleague is going to come around the room with a container. Please place your phones, tablets, and other electronic devices in it. They'll be returned to you after the tournament."

"He's kidding, right?" I ask Hamish.

"Sorry, lassie, but those are the rules due to a cheating scandal last year. There was this guy who had one of those fancy watches. You know, the kind that tracks your steps and heartbeat. Well, he had his girlfriend stand behind his competitors during matches. She would send coded messages to her boyfriend on his watch, telling him what tiles his opponents had. He would pretend to be looking at his watch to monitor his pulse, but in reality he was using the information his girlfriend sent to cheat."

"That's pretty clever," I said.

"Scrabble is serious business," Hamish says. "Especially when there's big prize money up for grabs."

"Phones, please." A man wearing a sweater vest two sizes too small for him thrusts a plastic container in front of me. His eyes are magnified by the oversized hot pink glasses perched on the end of his nose. He shakes the box, this time inches away from my face. "Phones."

I gulp. The success of my mission depends upon the phone Erich gave me. "But I'm expecting an important phone call."

Sweater vest man sighs. "Let me guess. Your grandmother is in the hospital on her deathbed."

"Well, um . . ."

He looks bored. "No, wait, I've got it. Your dog ate your homework. Maybe your backpack was stolen."

Not entirely sure what dogs and backpacks have to do with Scrabble, I venture a guess. "Are you by any chance a schoolteacher?"

"You're a clever one, aren't you?" He adjusts his glasses, which makes him look even more bug-eyed. "I've heard all the excuses. I know that your generation can't bear to be without your devices, but if you want to play Scrabble, you're going to have to say goodbye to it."

"Go on, lassie," Hamish urges.

I send Erich a quick text letting him know his phone has been confiscated, then reluctantly deposit it in the box. After the schoolteacher finishes his collection, he locks the container in a storage closet on the far side of the room.

Great. Lock-picking doesn't feature on my resume. Without the phone, all I can do is concentrate hard on what everyone looks like, then hope a sketch artist can turn my descriptions into something useful.

"Scrabblers, please take your assigned places for the warm-up round," the official announces.

"Your table is over there." Hamish points to the far end of the room.

I furrow my brow. "Where are you going to be?"

"Lucky for me, I don't have to go far."

"But I thought we'd be sitting together." I wring my hands. How am I supposed to keep a close eye on Hamish if we're on opposite sides of the room?

Hamish mistakes my concern for nerves for the match. "Don't worry, lassie. You'll do fine. I have every faith in you."

When I get to my table, my opponent is waiting for me. I extend my hand and introduce myself. Before she shakes my hand, she puts on a pair of pink furry mittens. When I ask her what her name is, she says, "I don't have a name."

"Everyone has a name," I say. "You would have needed a name to register for the tournament."

"Oh, *that* name." She removes her mittens, applies hand sanitizer, then puts them back on. "That name is Bob."

"Nice to meet you, uh, Bob."

There are two chairs at the table. One is facing the wall. The other is facing the direction where Hamish is sitting. Naturally, Bob sits in the seat facing Hamish. The very same seat I need to be in if I'm going to keep an eye on the Scotsman.

Bob does not want to switch chairs. I plead, I beg, I whine. Nothing works. Then I pull out the twenty Euro note from my purse—the only money I have, the one I almost spit a marshmallow into—and Bob is suddenly happy to cooperate.

I empty the bag of tiles onto the table so we can both confirm all hundred tiles are present and accounted for. "Ready to get started?"

"Just a minute." Bob reaches into her backpack and pulls out a roll of tinfoil. She fashions a hat out of it and places it on her head. "Ready."

You know, I'd like to say that's the strangest thing I've seen at a Scrabble tournament, but I'd be lying. Besides, Bob's hat is pretty jaunty—a cross between a beret and a Stetson. You wouldn't think you could combine those two styles of hats, but then again, who thought breeding a pit bull and a Chihuahua was a good idea? Turns out pithuahuas are adorable.

I struggle through the match, mostly because I spend more time trying to watch Hamish than I do looking at my tiles and maximizing my points. The only reason I end up winning is because Bob thinks that the colored spots on the board are bad luck, and avoids them at all costs. When I try to explain to her that she can earn double and triple scores using them, Bob puts her hands over her ears.

After the game is over, Bob removes her hat, taking care not to crumple it, and scurries off to the buffet table. I go find Hamish, making mental notes of all the people I pass.

"How was your match?" Hamish asks.

"I'm going to go with interesting."

"Those are the best kind," Hamish says. "Listen, I need to run to the gents. I'll meet you back here."

My eyes widen. "You're going to the bathroom?"

Hamish laughs. "That's what happens when you become old. The coffee runs right through you."

Erich and his stupid plan. Stick with Hamish. Follow Hamish. Don't lose sight of Hamish. Exactly how is this plan supposed to work if Hamish goes to the men's room?

CHAPTER 10
SCRABBLE NERDS

Time to get stealthy. Erich told me to keep Hamish in my sights, so I'm going to have to follow him to the men's room without him noticing me.

As part of my mission briefing, Erich showed me a map of the hotel. I know the ballroom is located in a separate wing. There's only one entrance into the ballroom from the hotel. Because of the cheating scandal last year, tournament officials guard that entrance, only admitting properly credentialed competitors inside. No family, friends, reporters, or secret agents allowed.

At the rear of the ballroom, a set of double doors opens up to a large corridor. The men's room is at one end of the corridor, the ladies' at the other end. You see how this is going to get tricky? Hamish will go in one direction, and as a woman, I should theoretically be going the other way.

Casually standing by the buffet table, I watch as Hamish traverses the ballroom. He moves slowly, pausing every few feet to catch his breath. Once he walks through the door to the corridor, I spring into action. I set my coffee cup down, then dart through the crowd. When I reach the door, I push it open slowly and poke my head around. As predicted, Hamish is still walking toward the men's room.

Fortunately, there's a group of Scrabble players huddled in the middle of the corridor, having an animated discussion about strategy. I use them as camouflage while Hamish makes his way to the restroom. While I'm standing there, I'm tempted to offer my own opinion about whether you should sacrifice your turn in order to exchange your tiles in the hopes of getting better ones. The answer is yes, by the way. From a short-term perspective, it seems foolhardy, but if you adopt a long-term perspective, it can be advantageous.

It's easier to think strategically when it comes to Scrabble. So much harder with relationships. With Scrabble, if you sacrifice your turn, you'll get zero points for that round, but you could end up winning the game. When it comes to love, if you make a grand gesture and sacrifice something important to you, there are two possible outcomes: live happily ever after or lose your heart. Losing a Scrabble game is one thing, but losing your heart . . . well, that's something else entirely. When that happens, you might just find yourself working in a mini-mart.

What should have been, is, I remind myself. *Acknowledge and accept the past. Time to move forward.*

It really is time to move forward. Forward past this group of Scrabblers. Hamish just went into the men's room. And now I need to . . . actually, I have no idea what to do next. Wait outside the men's room? That seems kind of stalky. Follow him into the men's room? Even stalkier. But when you're trying to save the world, you do what you got to do.

I open the door to the men's room a crack and peek in. On one side of the room are urinals. Fortunately, no one is doing his thing, if you know what I mean. Three stalls line the other side of the room. They have doors that run floor to ceiling, so I can't tell if they're occupied. Hamish is obviously in one of them, but I don't know which one.

As I creep inside, my sandals creak on the tiled floor. Slipping them off, I close the door quietly, then tiptoe over to the sinks. Leaning against them, I stare at the stalls. It feels a bit like a game show—what's behind door number one? Is it an older Scottish man who suffers from arthritis? Or is it an all-expense paid trip to Disneyland?

Turns out it's a young guy sporting a Scrabble t-shirt. The shirt is really cute, and I'm tempted to ask him if it comes in women's sizes. He looks surprised to see me. "Long line at the ladies' room," I whisper to him so that Hamish won't hear me. He motions to the stall he just exited, then leaves without washing his hands. Gross.

Okay, we know stall number one is empty now. That means Hamish is behind door number two or door number three. I check my hair in the mirror while I wait. It looks so much better loose than tied back in a bun.

I see door number two open out of the corner of my eye, and panic because I still haven't come up with a cover story to explain why I'm stalking Hamish in the men's room.

Phew. It's not Hamish. This time it's a middle-aged man. He's wearing a top hat, tuxedo, and bow tie. One of those people who treats Scrabble tournaments as formal events. I pretend to be a cleaner, scrubbing the sink with a paper towel. He seems nonplussed by my presence. He washes his hands. I give him an approving nod. Then he pulls a bottle of hand sanitizer out of his pocket and applies some. I'm impressed and mentally award him double points for personal hygiene.

Then he tosses his paper towel at the trashcan. He misses, but doesn't bother to pick it up off the floor. He knows it's on the floor, but deliberately chooses to leave it there for the custodial staff. Sure, his hands might be clean, but he's a jerk. I pick the towel up and throw it away. Then I spy what looks like a gum wrapper on the floor and toss that, too. You owe me, buddy.

That leaves door number three. I've decided what my cover story is when Hamish comes out—"This isn't this the women's room? But I could have sworn the icon on the door was wearing a skirt."

Totally believable, right? Such an easy mistake to make. It looks like a bathroom; it smells like a bathroom. Of course, there is the pesky matter of the urinals, which kind of give away the fact that this isn't the ladies' room. Anyway, I'll cross that bridge when I get to it.

I wait for what seems like an eternity. Then I begin to worry. It can't possibly take that long to go to the bathroom. Did Hamish have a heart attack or a stroke? Should I open the stall door and make sure he's okay? Do I break the door down?

Hamish might be a jewel thief, but he's still a nice guy. I have to do something. I knock gently on the door. "Hamish, are you okay?" When he doesn't answer, I knock more loudly. The door creaks open, apparently not latched properly.

When the door opens fully, I gasp. The stall is empty. Well, almost empty. Leaning against the tiled wall is Hamish's cane.

I run my fingers through my hair. Where did he go? Then, feeling a breeze, my eyes drift upward and I see an open window. It looks like my elderly, arthritic jewel thief has done a runner.

* * *

How does a senior citizen who needs a cane to get around pull himself up eight feet in order to crawl out a small window?

Well, duh, obviously he was faking the whole thing. Who knows if he's even Scottish.

I set my sandals down, climb onto the toilet seat, and peer out the window. It opens up to an alleyway. A dumpster is conveniently located underneath the window. There's no sign of Hamish, but that's not surprising as I spent nearly five minutes waiting in the men's room for him to appear. Plenty of time for him to shimmy out the window and disappear.

I scoop up Hamish's cane and hoist myself up to the windowsill. As I leap on top of the dumpster, I wonder if this is what it feels like to be a cat thief. I survey the alleyway, then startle when a rat runs across my feet. My bare feet. Why did I leave my sandals on the bathroom floor?

A debate rages inside me—climb back inside and retrieve my shoes or run down the alley in the hopes of spotting Hamish. I shake my head. Hamish is probably long gone by now. Get your shoes and retrieve Erich's phone. That's the sensible plan. But just as I reach up to grab hold of the windowsill, someone slams the window shut.

Time for another plan. Jump off the dumpster, walk down the alleyway dodging broken glass, rats, and garbage, then hope you can find a taxi on the main road. Sure, that will totally work cause taxis love picking up people who aren't wearing shoes and don't have any money on them. Sigh.

Not coming up with any better alternatives, I hop down from the dumpster. Fortunately, I make it through the alleyway unscathed. I'm now standing on a busy road. Hamish is nowhere to be seen, and taxis are non-existent. Turning right, I head back to the hotel, wincing when a woman runs over my toes with her baby stroller.

I hop up and down on one leg while waving the cane around wildly. "Son of a—"

"Isabelle, what in the world are you doing here?" a familiar voice says.

Erich is sitting at a cafe table, a pastry halfway to his mouth. He pushes back his chair and comes over to help me. "Here, sit down."

"Having a little coffee break?" I ask sarcastically.

He frowns. "Shouldn't you be playing Scrabble?"

"Yes, I should be, but things happened." I snatch up his pastry and take a bite.

"What things happened?"

"Hamish had to take a pee," I say, covering my mouth because it's full of the most delicious raspberry filling.

"I'm sorry, I'm not seeing the connection between

going to the bathroom and playing Scrabble."

"Hamish went into the men's room, the ordinary way through a door. Then he left the men's room, more unconventionally, through a window. So you see, there's no more Hamish and no more Scrabble." I polish off the pastry, then take a sip of Erich's coffee while he processes this.

"Why didn't you press the star key to let us know you needed urgent help?"

"Because the phone was confiscated. New tournament rules—no devices. How did you guys not know that was going to happen?"

Erich furrows his brow. He grabs his tablet and furiously taps on it. "That explains why, according to this tracker, you're still inside the hotel."

"Didn't you get my text? I sent you one when they took away the phone."

"No, nothing came through."

"And didn't you wonder why you hadn't received any pictures from me? That's what I was supposed to be doing during the tournament, snapping pictures."

"Between you and me, we've been having some technical difficulties on our end. They told me it was just a glitch and that your pictures were saved somewhere on the system. They promised a fix so we could access them." Erich scowls. "When I get my hands on the systems team—"

"Okay, enough hating on IT right now," I interject. "First things first. What are our next steps?"

Erich rubs the stubble on his jaw, then stares at the cane. "Can I see that?"

"He left it in the bathroom," I say as I hand it to him. "Speaking of which, we need to go back there to get my sandals."

"I was wondering about the bare feet." Erich runs his fingers along the length of the cane, then presses his fingernails on the groove near the handle. When the top of the cane opens and reveals an empty compartment, we both say "ooh" at the same time. "Looks like he kept the necklace in here. That's why I didn't find it when I searched his cabin."

"Do you think he gave the necklace to the fence in the men's room? He was in there for a few minutes before I worked up the nerve to go in."

"Did you see anyone else in there?" Erich asks.

"There were two men. The first was a young guy who didn't wash his hands. The second man was wearing a tux . . ." My eyes widen as I remember something. "Wait a minute, I think that was Bob wearing the tux."

"Who's Bob?"

"A woman I played against in the warm-up round."

Erich cocks his head to one side. "A woman named Bob in the men's room?"

Remembering the technique Erich taught me, I close my eyes and let the memories flood back. "That wasn't a gum wrapper I picked up. It was tin foil. Bob had a tinfoil hat. The man in the bathroom used hand sanitizer. So did Bob. There was pink lint on the tux. Bob wore pink mittens."

I take a deep breath and open my eyes. "Tuxedo man and Bob are the same person."

"Interesting," Erich says. "But how does it connect with Hamish?"

"I noticed Hamish brushing some lint off his shirt at the beginning of the tournament. I didn't pay much attention at the time, but I'm certain it was pink. Just like Bob's mittens. I think Bob and Hamish connected that morning, then made arrangements to do the exchange in the men's room during the break."

Erich gives me a huge smile, then kisses me on the cheek. "You're brilliant."

I'm startled by the sudden affection, but now's not the time to figure out what that's all about. Instead, I grab Erich's hand. "Come on, let's see if Bob is still at the hotel."

* * *

While we run around the block to the hotel entrance, I fill Erich in on what else I remember about Bob. He phones in a report to headquarters as we dash through the lobby. When we get to the ballroom, we're stopped by the obnoxious sweater vest-wearing official. He folds his arms across his chest. "Competitors only."

"I am a competitor." I reach up to show him the

lanyard around my neck, only to realize it's missing. "My badge must have fallen off."

The official shifts his position so that he's completely blocking the entrance to the ballroom. "Sure. Aliens abducted you and when they were beaming you on board, it fell off."

I fold my hands into a prayer position and implore him. "But I have to get inside."

"Sorry. No badge. No entry."

Fury boils up in me. Doesn't this guy know that global security is at stake? I try to push him aside, but there's a surprising amount of muscle underneath that sweater vest.

"Erich, want to give me a hand?" I snap.

Instead of answering, he walks away.

"Hey, where are you going?" I shout at him.

Without turning around, he crooks his finger behind him, motioning for me to follow him. I release my hands from the official's meaty arms. "Next time, buddy," I tell him, but he doesn't seem fazed by my idle threat.

Trailing behind Erich as he races through one hallway to the next, I fume. "Bob is going to get away and you think now is the time to explore the hotel?"

"Did you think there was only one way into the ballroom?" He holds open a door and ushers me inside the hotel's kitchen. "Follow me."

"If you can get in here so easily, why didn't you or

one of the organization's other agents pose as a cook or waiter? Wouldn't that have been an easier way to infiltrate the tournament?"

Erich stops so that someone carrying a heavy pot can get by. "We thought of that, but the kitchen staff can't spend all their time in the ballroom without raising suspicion."

If anyone is surprised to see us wander past their workstations, they don't show it. One of them even offers us an hors d'oeuvre. Of course, Erich carries himself with confidence and assurance. Maybe they think he's part of management, inspecting operations.

Erich pushes open a swinging door at the far end of the kitchen. "Ta da," he says when I see the ballroom on the other side.

The ballroom is quiet except for the rattle of Scrabble tiles. Everyone is focused on their boards, scouring their brains for high-scoring letter combinations. I search the room for Bob, but there's no sign of anyone in a tuxedo. "I don't see her. But maybe she has a new disguise."

Erich shakes his head. "No, Bob is long gone. Once she got the necklace, there wouldn't have been any reason for her to stick around."

I cock my head to one side. "Then why did you agree to come back here?"

He points at my feet. "You can't keep walking

around like that. Come on, let's go find your shoes."

* * *

I make Erich go into the bathroom to retrieve my sandals. I've had enough of men's rooms to last me a lifetime. As I'm slipping them back on my feet, Erich steadies me. "Let's grab some lunch."

"How can you be thinking about food right now? And don't say it's because of my blood sugar levels."

"Okay, we'll pretend that's not why. Anyway, I know this place that makes the best—"

"It better not be balkenbrij," I say.

"You've heard of it?"

"Before we got to Amsterdam, I looked up all the names of foods I won't eat in Dutch. That way, I won't end up getting something like balkenbrij. Animal heads? No, thank you."

As we walk back into the ballroom, Erich says, "Don't worry, this place we're going to serves German food. The strudel is out of this world."

"You come to the Netherlands and eat German food?"

"Well, the place is run by my aunt. I kind of have to stop by when I'm in town."

I halt in my tracks. "You're going to take me to meet your family?"

"In a way," Erich says. "Now, where's the phone?"

"In there." I jerk a finger at the storage closet. "But it's locked."

Erich pulls a lock pick out of his pocket and grins. "Not a problem. Can you create a distraction?"

"Sure." I walk over to a table on the other side of the room and stand behind one of the competitors. I whistle, then say in a loud voice that carries across the ballroom, "Would you look at that. This woman has ten tiles on her rack."

The uproar that ensues is predictable. Having more than seven tiles is the most blatant form of cheating there is in Scrabble. I feel horrible about what I did to the woman. She only had the regulation amount of tiles, but Erich did say to create a distraction, and I couldn't think of anything else in the spur of the moment.

I push my way through the angry mob that's forming around the poor lady and rush back to Erich. "Grab Hamish's phone too," I say. "It's the one with the tartan cover."

We quickly exit the ballroom, much to the sweater vest official's surprise. "How did you get in there?" he yells at our retreating backs.

During the car ride to the restaurant, I can't stop laughing about our escape. "James Bond has nothing on us."

"James Bond probably has a better IT department," Erich grumbles as he pulls up in front of a nondescript building. There's a small German flag stuck in a planter by the door and a tattered poster of Berlin taped on the inside of one of the windows. When we enter the restaurant, the lights are off, and the place is deserted.

"I guess German food isn't that popular in the Netherlands," I say.

"That's the way we like it," a woman's voice says.

I squint in the darkness, trying to make out who's speaking, but all I can see are cobwebs.

"Bring your friend back to the kitchen," she says.

Her voice is deep and raspy. It sends chills down my spine. Am I about to be eliminated because it's my fault that the mission failed?

Erich puts his hand on the small of my back. "It's okay," he says in a soft, reassuring voice.

As he guides me into the kitchen, the lights suddenly come on, blinding me. I put my hands over my eyes and let out a tiny whimper. The bright lights. I know what that means—they're going to interrogate me before I'm eliminated.

"For goodness' sake, dim those lights," the woman barks at someone. "The girl can't see."

Once the lights are adjusted, I can make out a woman standing behind a metal food prep counter. She's the spitting image of Frau Albrecht, from her beady eyes down to her incessant knuckle cracking.

"Is that who I think it is?" I whisper to Erich.

He murmurs in my ear, "No, but I think they might have been twins separated at birth."

"Silence!" Frau Albrecht's doppelganger slams a meat cleaver on the counter, sending reverberations through the room.

Erich calmly introduces us. "Isabelle, this is Aunt C."

"This is your aunt?" I ask.

"No, this is Aunt C. 'C' as in chief. That's her official designation," Erich explains.

"Sit down." Aunt C points at two wooden stools, then gives me an appraising look. "So this is the girl I've heard so much about."

"I think you mean woman," I mumble.

Erich puts his fingers to his lips. I probably should keep quiet, but my grandmother's ring glints in the light. I feel courage flowing through me. I lean across the counter and glare at the older woman. "What exactly have you heard about me?"

She turns to stir a pot on the stove, ignoring my question.

"Oh, I get it. You've read my file. You think you know everything there is to know about me." I tap my chest. "But you'll never know everything. You'll never know what's in my mind and heart."

Aunt C cackles. She looks at Erich and says, "You were right. She is feisty." Then she sets a bowl of soup in front of me. "Eat."

"I'm not hungry."

She chuckles. "Don't worry. There isn't any organ meat in there. Just chicken thighs."

"Try it," Erich urges.

"It's good," I say begrudgingly after sampling a small spoonful.

"Good. I'm glad you like it, especially considering it's your last meal."

I spit out my soup. "You really are going to kill me."

"Feisty and imaginative," Aunt C says as she wipes off the counter. She looks at me and her expression softens. "I meant that this is your last meal with Erich. You won't see him again after today."

I look over at Erich, but he's concentrating on his soup. Aunt says something to him in German. He nods, then carries his empty bowl to the sink. He walks back to me and kisses my forehead. "Take care of yourself, Isabelle."

Then he walks out of the door, and he's gone. Gone forever.

CHAPTER 11
POTATO ALLERGIES

It's hard to believe it's been a month since the Scrabble tournament. A month since the mission failed because Hamish had to go to the men's room. A month since I said goodbye to Erich at that strange German restaurant.

Since then, we've had four cruises up and down the Rhine River, and I've really gotten into the groove of being a tour manager. Even Frau Albrecht grudgingly admitted that I was doing a satisfactory job. Okay, she didn't say "satisfactory." She said, "You're not utterly disappointing," but that's close enough for me. Sophia and I have even come to a semi-truce. In fact, she's seemed to really warm up to me after I told her I wasn't planning on renewing my contract. The job she's had her heart set on will be all hers next season.

Admittedly, the week I spent with Erich was

chaotic and I was anxious much of the time, but I felt so alive. It made me realize that being a tour manager isn't what my future holds. I'm not sure what the universe has in store for me, but it's certainly not working on a riverboat or at a mini-mart.

Erich reminded me that there are positive attributes to anxiety. People who constantly worry about what could go wrong are better at responding to threats because their brain processes danger more efficiently. Given his German love of efficiency, I can see why he liked that particular fact. He also pointed out that if you spend a lot of time ruminating about things, you tend to be more intelligent. There are days where I'd happily trade some IQ points for not constantly obsessing about things, but I'm learning to find peace with how my brain is wired.

We're currently in Amsterdam, at the start of a seven-day cruise to Basel, Switzerland. The latest group of passengers is waiting for me in the lounge, ready to hear my welcome presentation. I calmly walk up to the podium, attach the mike on my lapel, and greet them warmly. "How's everyone doing tonight? We're delighted to have you aboard the *Abenteuer*. I met most of you when you checked in, but for those who don't know me, my name is Isabelle Martinez and I'll be your tour manager on this cruise."

Sophia pipes up from the back of the room. "There isn't anything about this cruise that Isabelle doesn't know. You're lucky to have her."

I smile at her, then click through the slides. The presentation goes smoothly. No embarrassing photos, no questions I can't answer.

When the session is over, several passengers approach me to ask about excursions near Breisach—should they go on the cycling trip through the Black Forest or explore the medieval village of Colmar? They're delighted when I tell them they can do both.

I notice an older gentleman standing off by himself at the edge of the group, presumably waiting to speak with me. His jet-black hair is pulled back into a ponytail, and he's dressed in dark jeans and an oversized houndstooth jacket. The curled tips of his handlebar mustache are impressive. How exactly do guys do that? Do they use tiny curling irons? Special styling products?

The group asks a few more questions about the best desserts to order once we get to Germany. "The strudel, without a doubt," I tell them. "It's my absolute favorite."

When they wander off, I turn to the mustached man. "Can I help you, sir?"

There's something familiar about him. He's wearing dark sunglasses indoors at night, so maybe he's some sort of celebrity who thinks sunglasses can conceal his identity.

The man clears his throat, then says in a heavy Russian accent, "Ready for another adventure?"

"Oh, yes, there will be plenty or adventures on the

cruise. I was just telling those folks about the cycling excursion. And if you're not afraid of heights, you can take the cable car in Koblenz."

"Those don't sound very exciting," he says. "I was thinking of an adventure of a different kind."

An adventure of another kind? Is he propositioning me? I did not sign up for this. Attempting to defuse the situation, I say, "You know what, sir, why don't I get you one of the brochures and you can have a look at the excursions we have available?"

As I turn to get a brochure from the table, he grabs my hand. What does this guy think he's doing? My adrenaline kicks in, and I get ready to stomp on his foot with my heel.

"I see that you're still feisty," he says as he removes his sunglasses.

I find myself staring into a pair of icy-blue eyes, and my heart flutters. "Erich? Is that you?"

* * *

Except for the eyes, the man standing in front of me looks completely different from the Erich I knew. But the way his fingers felt as he grabbed my hand, that was oh so familiar.

"What are you doing here, Erich?" I put my hand on my stomach, trying to quiet the butterflies in it. "And why are you in disguise?"

"Shush, don't use that name. It's Andrei Petrov now." He put his sunglasses back on. "A Russian businessman on vacation."

"This is crazy. Next thing you know, you'll be telling me you're here on a mission."

"I'm always on a mission. You know that," he says. "Why don't we go somewhere more private and I'll explain."

I follow Erich to his cabin in a daze. I was getting into a stable routine aboard the boat. Boring, but stable. I thought I wanted more excitement in my life, but now I'm not sure. When Erich opens the door, I'm so out of sorts that I don't even care if anyone notices that I'm going into a passenger's room.

Reminding myself to breathe slowly, I survey his accommodations. "I see you got a stateroom again."

"I'm not sure I could cope with a budget cabin after I've experienced this," Erich says wryly.

After motioning for me to sit on the small settee, he proceeds to take off his disguise. First, he removes his sunglasses, then peels off his fake beard and mustache. Next, he takes off his wig, revealing his natural blond hair. Hair I'm longing to run my fingers through.

As soon as Erich hangs up his suit jacket and unbuttons the top of his shirt, his posture transforms. Gone is the stooped over Russian businessman. In his place is the German equivalent of James Bond—confident, sexy, and dangerous.

"Are you hungry? I could order room service," he says.

"I'm fine." I cock my head to one side. "Why are you still talking with a Russian accent?"

"It helps to stay in character."

I hug one of the throw cushions to my chest. "Were you playing a character on the last cruise? Are you even German?"

Erich—if that's even his name—doesn't answer. "Well, I'm hungry." He picks up the phone and orders grilled fish. Not steak like before. Did he even like steak or did he eat it because his fake German persona was supposed to? What do I really know about this man standing in front of me?

I guess I said that last bit out loud, because Erich says, "You knew more about me than most people." The tone of his voice is harsh, bitter almost. He pours himself a shot of vodka and downs it. "I started to care for you and . . ."

He pauses to refill his glass. His hand is grasping the bottle so tightly that I'm scared it's going to shatter. "What a mistake that night was. I should have never let that happen."

Before he can down his drink, I walk over and place my hand on his arm. "You don't think I regret that night, too? But it happened. We kissed, and it was incredible."

Erich sets his glass down so quickly that I jump back. He grabs hold of me, pulling me into his arms.

His hands run up and down my back. "It was incredible, wasn't it?" he murmurs in my ear.

My breath hitches in my chest as I breathe in his familiar scent. He lowers his mouth and his lips brush against mine. I twine my fingers through his hair, pulling him closer to me. My heartbeat quickens as I wait for him to kiss me again.

"Room service," a voice calls out.

Erich turns his face from mine, and says loudly, "Leave it by the door, please."

"How could they grill a fish so fast?" I wonder out loud.

Erich releases me, then sits on the edge of the bed and puts his head in his hands. "I told Aunt C that it was a bad idea to have us work together again."

Not knowing what to say, I go to the door to get the room service. Checking to make sure no one is in the hall first, I grab the cart and wheel it into the room. I set his fish on the table, then pour myself my own shot of vodka. Then I remind myself that I don't normally drink shots, and set the glass aside.

Erich looks up at me. "I'm sorry, but this is what you do to me. You cause me to lose control of my emotions. And that's a liability in my line of work."

I sit on the bed next to him and take his hand in mine. "When I was working in intelligence, I dated someone who was a field operative. We both had to keep so many secrets from each other that it destroyed our relationship."

"So you understand." He caresses my hand gently. "Whatever this is between us, we can't pursue it."

"Agreed. That's why I pulled away from you that night on deck. Believe me, I didn't want to, but I knew it was for the best." I take a deep breath, then point at the table. "Your fish is getting cold. You should eat."

He nods. "Okay, then I'll tell you about our mission."

"*Our* mission?" I shake my head. "After I botched the last mission—"

Erich interrupts me. "You didn't botch anything. We had bad intel. If we had known they were going to confiscate your phone, we would have come up with a different plan. Not to mention how our IT department screwed up. What a disaster."

"But the men's room," I say. "I was standing outside while Hamish made the exchange with Bob."

"Again, bad intel on our part. We were operating under the assumption that the exchange would be done during the Scrabble match, not in the bathroom."

"Well, when you put it that way . . ."

Erich walks over to the table and uncovers his plate. "Do you want to hear about our new mission?"

"Sure." I rub my hands together, eager to hear the details.

He takes a bite of his meal, then frowns. "I hate fish."

"The mission," I prompt.

"Oh, yeah, I think you're going to like this one. We need you to pretend to be my fiancée."

* * *

"You want me to be your fake fiancée?" I burst out laughing. "That's the most ridiculous thing I've ever heard."

"That's not what Aunt C thinks," Erich says. "She believes that the mission has the best chance of success if you go undercover as my fiancée."

"Perhaps she's pulling your leg?"

Erich shakes his head. "Aunt C wouldn't joke about something like that."

"Yeah, no kidding," I say. "She didn't strike me as someone who has a sense of humor. But I suppose people who work for the organization don't. I guess it comes with the territory."

Erich protests. "I have a sense of humor."

"You've told me one bad joke since I've known you. That does *not* constitute a sense of humor." I shake my head. "The few times I've heard you laugh, your eyes don't light up. It's like you're laughing because you think you're supposed to, not because you're actually having a light-hearted moment."

"That's not true."

"Really? When's the last time you laughed so hard you couldn't stop? Not just a brief chuckle, but a full-on belly laugh."

Erich lowers his eyes and his shoulders slump ever so slightly. "I haven't had much to laugh about lately," he says quietly.

"I'm sorry," I say gently, feeling awful that I started this line of conversation. Like the rest of us, Erich probably has his own history full of painful memories.

"Nonsense," he says crisply, fixing his icy-blue eyes on mine. "Nothing to be sorry about. Now, shall we talk about the mission?"

You can't make someone talk about something they don't want to. And, to be honest, I'm not sure I want to know what's happened to Erich in the past. Could I handle it?

I fold my hands in my lap and adopt an attentive pose. "Sure, go ahead. I'm all ears."

He pushes his plate away. He's only taken a couple of bites of his fish. I guess the real Erich is more of a red meat guy. Or is the real Erich a lover of seafood and he's only pretending not to enjoy his meal? My head is swimming, trying to discern what's real and what's not.

"There will be a black-tie party at a historic mansion in Basel," Erich says, interrupting my thoughts. "It's being held to raise money for endangered animals. I'll be attending, posing as Andrei Petrov, an eccentric and reclusive Russian businessman. He hasn't been seen in public in over twenty years, which makes pretending to be him easier."

"What kind of business is Andrei in?" I ask.

"Potato peelers," Erich says.

I cock my head to the side. "So not a rich businessman then?"

"There's a lot of money in potato peelers."

"Are they encrusted in diamonds? Plated in twenty-four carat gold?"

"No, just ordinary metal." He shrugs. "What can I say? People eat a lot of potatoes in Russia. They need peelers."

"Okay, so how does a fiancée fit in?"

"Well, Andrei recently became engaged to a beautiful, young Russian woman. Fortunately, she's also a recluse. They met on a dating app. It's really a classic 'opposites attract' love story. His fortune is based on potatoes. She's allergic to them."

"How do I fit in?"

"You're similar in looks to Andrei's fiancée."

"But you said she's beautiful." Yeah, I admit it, I'm fishing for compliments.

Erich gives me an appreciative look. "You definitely check that box."

I repress a smile and try not to let my thoughts stray too far from the mission at hand. "But I'm not allergic to potatoes. I eat them all the time. In fact, I had French fries for lunch."

"Were they the shoestring ones? I had those the

last time I was on board the *Abenteuer.* I love the seasoning salt the chef puts on them."

"Uh-huh. The salt is what makes them so addictive. I have them practically every day." I pat my stomach. "It feels like I've gained a lot of weight since I started this job."

"Doesn't look like it to me," he says as his eyes sweep over me.

"It's the suit," I say. "The material is stretchy. That's the only good thing I can say about this uniform, really. What I wouldn't give to wear normal clothes again."

"You'll get to wear an evening gown to the party," Erich says.

"Ooh . . . what does it look like? What color? Is it strapless?" Then I mentally slap myself. I'm not in a boutique shopping for dresses. I'm sitting here with a spy who's concocted the most bizarre cover story for an undercover mission that he wants me to be part of. "Never mind, let's get back to the fiancée potato allergy thing. Exactly how does this all fit into your latest save-the-world plan?"

"Okay, so when Andrei fell madly in love with Svetlana—"

"Svetlana, huh?" I repeat her name a few times. "Okay, I can live with that."

"Anyway, he asked her to marry him and she agreed on one condition—that he sell his potato peeler business."

"Wow, that's asking a lot," I say. "Quite a sacrifice our Andrei is making for love."

"He probably thinks he doesn't deserve her." Erich clears his throat. "Anyway, at the party, Andrei is going to the party to meet with a sheikh who wants to buy the potato peeler business."

"They have a lot of unpeeled potatoes in the Middle East?"

"You'd be surprised. It's a real problem."

"If I didn't know better, I'd almost think that was a joke," I say.

"Maybe it is," Erich says with a faint twinkle in his eye. "Anyway, the sheikh also happens to be an arms dealer."

"You mean *the* arms dealer? The one who is going to give Nouveau Rouge Order weapons in exchange for the necklace that Hamish stole? The same terrorist group who is going to be responsible for the attack on the United Nations?"

Erich nods. "That's the one."

I rub my temples. "Let me see if I've got this straight. Hamish stole an emerald necklace. Hamish put the emerald in a secret compartment in his cane. Hamish then sold the necklace to the fence, Bob, in the men's room at a Scrabble tournament."

"You're a hundred for a hundred so far," Erich says. "Keep going."

"Okay, Bob then passed the necklace to the terrorists. Now a member of the Nouveau Rouge

Order is going to this party to exchange the necklace for the weapons."

Erich nods. "That's correct."

I run my fingers through my hair, then grumble when I remember it's still pinned up in a bun. "So what is the sheikh going to do with the necklace?"

"Give it to Andrei in exchange for the potato peeler business."

"Hasn't anyone ever heard of cashier's checks?" I muse. Then I look at Erich. "But if you're hanging around for the sheikh to give you this necklace, isn't it too late? Won't the terrorists already have their hands on the weapons?"

"Tell you what, why don't we save that part of the plan for another day," he says. "I haven't slept in thirty-seven hours and I need to get some shut-eye."

As Erich escorts me to the door, I say, "Aren't there other agents who could pose as Svetlana? Surely someone else has to resemble her. Someone with actual field experience. Why in the world would you want to involve me?"

"Well, you speak Russian fluently, which is critical. You score high on agility tests and you can run fast." When I furrow my brow, he says, "It will make sense when I tell you more about the plan."

"I still think there have to be other people who can speak Russian and are athletic."

"There are. We do have a back-up plan in place," he admits. "But . . ."

"But what?"

"We have chemistry together. People will believe that we're in love." Erich pauses, then adds, "At least, that's what Aunt C thinks."

"What do you think?"

Erich shoves his hands in his pockets. I think we make a good team."

"Andrei and Svetlana," I say. "That has a nice ring to it."

"So, you'll do it?" Erich asks.

"Da," I say, answering him in Russian.

CHAPTER 12
CRAWLING THROUGH
CARDBOARD BOXES

Why in the world did I say yes to Erich's latest hare-brained scheme? Me, posing as a Russian billionaire's fiancée—ridiculous, right?

There are three big issues with his plan. First of all, it's been ages since I've spoken Russian. I'm pretty rusty, but Erich is convinced that it'll come back to me.

Second, I have to pretend to be allergic to potatoes. Erich told me I should avoid all potato products until the mission is over. That way it'll be second nature to me to say no to all things potato, because, heaven forbid, they serve potato puffs at the party and I snarf them down, blowing my cover. It seemed logical when Erich explained to me, but giving up my daily shoestring French fries from now until the mission?

That's a big ask.

The third issue, and the most terrifying one, is having to fake being attracted to Erich. How am I supposed to do that?

Okay, I know what you're thinking—Isabelle, this isn't something you're going to have to fake. You're totally attracted to him. Everything about him drives you crazy. Whenever you're in the same room with him, you want to brush your lips against his, feel his strong arms enveloping you in an embrace . . .

Okay, enough of that train of thought. You're right. I'm attracted to Erich. End of story. But we're going to have to be physically affectionate with each other during this party, standing close to each other, holding hands, and the occasional kiss. One little peck on the cheek and it's going to be hard to rein in my desire for him.

So why did I agree to this? Is it because I want more excitement in my life? Or is it because I want to spend more time with Erich? Or both?

I push these thoughts out of my head. I have guests waiting for me in the reception area, eager to head out on this morning's excursion. As I pass Erich on the way to the dining room to grab a to-go coffee, he says quietly in Russian, "My cabin tonight."

"Da," I reply, wishing it was already this evening.

It was a rough day at Kinderdijk, a UNESCO World Heritage Site south of Amsterdam. As we toured the open-air windmill museum, two of the guests decided it would be a good idea to take a picture with some goats. They bent down to pose with the animals. One of the goats decided that the woman's long brown hair looked like it would make a good snack. When he started chomping on it, she yelped.

That might have been the end of the story, but she was wearing a wig and when she tried to extricate herself, there was a struggle. The goat won. He placidly continued to chew on the wig while she screamed and threatened to sue the cruise line. By the time we recovered her wig, rinsed it out in the bathroom sink, and calmed everyone down, we were two hours late boarding the boat. Naturally, Frau Albrecht blamed me.

We finally get underway for the overnight sail to our next destination, and I head to Erich's cabin. As usual, I make sure the coast is clear before I enter. The last thing I need is for people to think I'm having inappropriate relations with a passenger. The rumors about me having an affair with Erich were bad enough. Imagine what it would be like if they started talking about Andrei and me.

"She's slept with two different passengers," they'd say.

Concerned that they'd think I was a complete hussy, I'd want to correct them—"It's only one passenger. Erich and Andrei are the same guy. And I didn't sleep with him." Of course, that wouldn't fly. I can't break Erich's latest cover. So it's better if the rumors don't get started in the first place.

When I walk into Erich's cabin, he pulls me toward him and kisses me on both cheeks.

"I thought we weren't doing this," I say, squirming out of his arms.

"We're not doing it for real," he says. "Just practicing so that we look natural at the party."

"Why don't we focus on the mission details?" I suggest.

"Fine." He pulls a folder out of the desk drawer. "This is a dossier on Svetlana. While she hasn't been seen in public in a few years, you need to be prepared in case there's anyone at the party who knows her. If they notice any differences in appearance, you'll need to attribute it to cosmetic surgery. Despite being a young woman, she has her plastic surgeon on speed dial."

I flip through the pages in the folder. "She's a pet groomer?"

"Uh-huh, specializes in hamsters."

"I didn't know hamsters needed to be groomed."

Erich leans against the desk. "The rich and famous have their hamsters flown to her on their private planes for blowouts. Hamsters with sleek, shiny fur are the latest thing among the one percent."

"I can't imagine they enjoy that. I hope she uses a cool setting." Erich gives me a look and I hold up my hand. "Don't worry, I'll disguise my feelings about blow drying hamsters when the time comes."

"The other thing you need to do is practice your Russian. That's all we should speak with one another from this point forward." He switches to Russian, saying, "Then there's your agility training."

"I've been wondering about that. What kind of training are you talking about?"

"You need to practice squeezing into small spaces and maneuvering around in them."

I raise my eyebrows. "And here I thought my job was to look pretty on your arm and talk about hamsters."

"Yes, and crawling through an air-conditioning duct." Erich unrolls a blueprint. "See this here? This is in a small office off the reception hall. It won't be in use during the event. There's a vent in the ceiling where you can access the ductwork. You'll follow the ducting from here to a vent in the library. Once you're in position, you'll record the meeting between the sheikh and the terrorist. That will give us the evidence we need to bring the Nouveau Rouge Order down."

"Why can't you do this?" I ask as I study the blueprint.

"My shoulders are too broad to fit through the ducting."

I pause for a moment to take in his physique. I do like those shoulders of his, but right now I wish they were a lot narrower. "Okay, well, it sounds easy enough," I say. "It looks like a straight shot from the office to the library."

Erich purses his lips. "Well, not exactly. When the owner of the building decided to have the air-conditioning system updated, he awarded the contract to his nephew."

"I don't follow."

"Well, the nephew was in the midst of making a career change. He used to have a company that designed rat mazes."

"That's a thing?"

"Sure, but not very lucrative, hence the move into air conditioning." Erich traces a zigzag line on the blueprint with his finger. "He installed the ducting to resemble a maze. There are lots of tight twists and turns, not to mention dead ends. Extremely inefficient."

"So basically, I have to pretend I'm a rat," I say. "And here I thought being a spy was such a glamorous job."

"Glamorous? Hah. You'd be surprised how much paperwork there is."

I walk over to the settee and sit down. Patting the spot next to me, I ask, "How did you become a spy, anyway?"

"I filled out an application. It's pretty much like any job."

"Being a spy is definitely not like any other job," I say. "I worked at a mini-mart. They were so desperate for workers that, if you so much as glanced at the application, they hired you on the spot."

"Admittedly, the secret agent recruitment process is a bit more in-depth. You attend an assessment center where they put you through a series of personality assessments, role-playing exercises, and simulations."

"Did any of the simulations cover crawling through air-conditioning ducts?"

When Erich laughs, I notice that it seems less forced. "Not exactly."

"So that's it. You take a few tests, and presto, you're a spy?"

"No, if you pass the assessment center, then there are extensive background checks. I'm sure you went through something similar to get security clearance when you worked in intelligence."

"Yeah, it was really thorough," I say. "They talked to my family and friends, checked out my bank accounts, and asked me about my overseas travels."

"One of the last things they do is have a stranger approach you on a bus or train, something like that." Erich rubs his jaw. It looks raw, and I wonder if he's having a reaction to the adhesive he uses for his fake beard. "They engage you in conversation and see how much personal information you disclose."

"Let me guess, you aced that test. No one could accuse you of blabbing too much about yourself."

"True," he says. "In my line of work, it's an asset."

"That must be harder in your personal life," I muse.

Erich gives me a wry look. "It's easy when you don't have a personal life."

* * *

"So, this is it," Erich says. It's the last evening of the cruise. We've just docked in Basel. Erich and I are on the sun deck, leaning against the railing and watching the water lap against the side of the boat. "I'll be disembarking with the rest of the passengers tomorrow morning. Then I'll meet you back here in two weeks' time for the black-tie event."

"After spending each night with you training for the mission, it's going to be strange to go back to normal for two weeks," I say.

"You'll still need to prepare," Erich says. "Practice your Russian, avoid potatoes, and keep crawling through cardboard boxes."

I laugh as he reminds me of the simulations he set up in his cabin. Somehow, he managed to procure boxes that are the exact dimensions of the air-conditioning duct I'll be climbing through, and set up a mini-maze on the floor of his cabin. Housekeeping thought it was very strange, but he explained that he was a cat in a past life and had an affinity for boxes. They still thought it was odd, but at least they decided he was a harmless eccentric.

"You only have two weeks before the mission," he cautions me. "You sail back up to Amsterdam, then return here to Basel. You need to keep focused."

I gaze into the distance, watching the sunset. It's not going to be the same without Erich on board. It's amazing how quickly I've become accustomed to spending every hour I'm not working with him.

Erich clears his throat, then pulls a small velvet box out of his jacket pocket. The last time he gave me jewelry, it was the Scrabble charm bracelet. This one is smaller; the size of box that would normally contain a ring. When he bends down, for a moment, I think he's going to propose. Where did that crazy thought come from? But instead he picks up a napkin that the breeze has blown our way.

He gets back to his feet and thrusts the box into my hands. "This is for when I see you next."

When I open it, I gasp. "I hope this is fake."

Erich removes the ring and slips it on my finger. "Don't worry, it's not a real diamond. It's what's inside the diamond that's really valuable." He shows me how to press the band so that the diamond and its setting pop open, revealing a miniature recording device.

That's when the reality of what I'm supposed to do hits me. Up until now, it's seemed like a game. I mean, I've been crawling around in cardboard boxes, for goodness' sake. Something kids or cats do. Not something people do if they're about to embark on a mission to stop the Nouveau Rouge Order.

Are you kidding? Me stopping terrorists?

I begin to feel that sense of overwhelming doom that signals the start of a massive anxiety attack. My heart pounds, my skin grows clammy, and I feel faint. I clutch the railing while repeating every mantra I can think of to calm my breathing. Nothing works.

"Isabelle, are you okay?" Erich catches me by the waist when I start to collapse. "What's going on? Talk to me."

His touch calms me, and after a while, I feel able to speak again.

"I can't do this, Erich. I'm sorry."

"Of course you can," he says.

I pull away from him. "Look at me. I'm already panicking. Imagine what would happen if I had an anxiety attack while crawling through the ductwork."

Erich cradles my face. "What can I do to help?"

"Nothing." I remove the ring and hand it back to him. "There's nothing you can do. You're going to have to go with the back-up plan. I'm sorry."

"You have nothing to be sorry about." Just like in the German restaurant, he kisses my forehead. "Take care of yourself, Isabelle."

As he walks away, my eyes tear up. This is the second time I've said goodbye to Erich. I thought the first time was bad, but I think this one might just break me.

CHAPTER 13
THE UNDERCOVER PASSENGER

It's been a week since Erich and I said goodbye. I can't tell you how many times I wanted to call him and tell him I changed my mind. Sure, they had another agent ready to step in and take my place, but Erich and I had trained for a week for this mission. Was she as prepared as I am? Would people believe that she and Erich were in love? Do they have chemistry together? When he kisses her, will he forget all about me?

Wow, am I ever self-centered. All I seem to care about is Erich being with another woman, not the actual mission. This is supposed to be about stopping terrorists. My personal feelings about Erich are irrelevant in the larger scheme of things. I have to keep reminding myself of that.

Sophia nudges me. "Are you okay? You seem distracted."

I snap out of my self-indulgent daydreaming and smile at her. "Yeah, I'm fine."

"If you ever need to talk . . ." she says tentatively.

"Thanks, but I'm not sure talking will help," I say, fidgeting with my charm bracelet.

"Well, if you change your mind, you know where I am."

Now that she knows she's getting the tour manager job for sure next season, Sophia has been so much fun to work with. She jokes around and shares stories about the crew. My favorites are the ones about Frau Albrecht's background. Who knew the woman had such an interesting life before working aboard a riverboat. The fact that Frau Albrecht was on the German national synchronized swimming team when she was younger amazes me. But her dreams of turning pro were brought to a halt when she developed a terrible allergy to chlorine. Just touching a drop of pool water caused her to break out in a terrible rash. Kind of makes you wonder why she wasn't more sympathetic to my allergy to nylons. Was it because her hopes for the future were crushed? Is that why she likes to see other people suffer?

As if she can sense me thinking about her, Frau Albrecht comes out of the back room and inspects the reception desk. "Isabelle, straighten up those welcome packs. We're ready to begin boarding."

Sophia prints out the passenger manifest while I stack the welcome packs.

Frau Albrecht signals for the doors to be opened. "Let's make sure check-in goes quickly and efficiently." Then she lowers her voice and adds, "Someone may be undercover on this cruise."

Sophia scowls. "Again? It wasn't that long ago we had someone undercover. That guy was a real nightmare to please."

I startle, knocking a stapler and pen holder on the floor. They knew about Erich being an undercover agent? And now there's going to be another spy on board?

"Clean that up, Isabelle. Everything needs to look shipshape," Frau Albrecht says. "We can't afford a bad rating."

As I'm scooping up the pens, I look up at the older woman and ask, "Why would an undercover agent rate you?"

"Because that's their job." She shakes her head. "Get your head out of the clouds. You need to be sharp. My bonus depends on it."

Now I'm really lost. The organization is giving out bonuses? Does this mean that Frau Albrecht is also an agent? Is Sophia one too? My head is spinning. I sit down and fan myself with a piece of paper.

"Did your source in Head Office give you any idea what they look like?" Sophia asks Frau Albrecht.

"All I know is that it's an American woman who will be traveling with a relative. Her last assignment was on a cruise from Miami to Italy. This will be her first time on a riverboat."

"How old is she?" Sophia asks.

"Retirement age," Frau Albrecht says. "Oh, and one other thing, apparently she loves to dance. But I don't know if she'll be on board this cruise or the next one."

"I hate not knowing." Sophia smooths down her skirt. "But I guess that's the point. You never know which passenger Head Office has sent undercover to evaluate the crew's performance, so you have to make sure you give excellent service to everyone."

"Wait a minute," I say. "This woman you're talking about—she's like a mystery shopper in a store?"

"Correct. Haven't you been paying attention?" Frau Albrecht snaps. "Just be on the lookout for someone who fits the description, then make sure to give her the VIP treatment."

Relieved that Frau Albrecht and Sophia aren't talking about secret spy agents—and feeling slightly stupid that I didn't figure it out before—I relax into welcoming the guests on board. Sophia and I even make a bit of a game out of it as we try to identify who the undercover passenger is.

During a lull, I go into the back to print out more handouts. Naturally, the copier jams and I spend ten minutes pulling paper out of the feeder tray. While I'm trying to get toner off my fingers, Sophia rushes in.

"Hurry up and get out front. I think the undercover passenger is here." Sophia hands me a wet wipe, then ticks items off on her fingers. "She's American. She's traveling with her niece. She arrived in Italy in May on a cruise ship from Miami."

Sophia is practically jumping up and down by this point. She grabs my hand and squeezes it, getting toner on herself. "And get this—she asked me if there was a dance floor. She wants to practice her tango."

"Clean up and let's go give her the VIP treatment," I say, tossing her the pack of wet wipes.

When I see who's standing at the reception desk, I do a double take. "Celeste? I thought you were in Greece."

The woman beams at me. "Surprise!" Then she scoots around the desk and envelops me in a hug.

"You two know each other?" Sophia asks.

"Remember how I was telling you I won tickets for a transatlantic cruise? That's how my friend Mia and I got to Europe," I say to Sophia. "Well, that's when I met Celeste. She kind of adopted us, along with Ginny, this other girl we met on board."

Celeste pinches my cheeks. "I like to think of myself as you girls' fairy godmother. Whenever one of you has troubles with your love life, I'm there to help out."

I smile warmly at Celeste. She's like a surrogate mother and eccentric Dear Abby rolled into one. Her advice is often a bit strange, but always heartfelt.

"Now, come meet my niece, Olivia. She's been staying with me in Greece." Celeste leads me over to a woman about my age who has a bemused look on her face. Her tousled black bob, perfectly applied make-up, and stylish clothes make me feel positively frumpy with my tight bun and ill-fitting uniform.

"Olivia met a wonderful guy—he owns a taverna near my villa," Celeste says after she introduces us. "He makes the most divine baklava. But his mother . . . well, let's just say that I thought it would be good for Olivia to get away for a while."

Olivia rolls her eyes at her aunt. "Do we need to tell everyone my life story within two minutes of meeting them?" She turns to me and says, "You should have heard what she told the taxi driver. Did he really need to know how old I was when I learned to walk?"

"It's such a coincidence that you would go on a cruise on the same boat I'm working on," I say to them.

"It's no coincidence, dear. The universe told me your love life is at a crossroads." Celeste loops her hand through my arm. "I'm here to help."

* * *

When I walk into the lounge later that evening, Celeste is perched atop the baby grand piano, belting out show tunes. Frau Albrecht is convinced that Celeste is the undercover passenger, so she's ordered the staff to give her the VIP treatment. That includes having the bartender ready to refill Celeste's water glass should she look even the slightest bit parched and a waiter holding a tray of chocolate-covered marshmallows in case hunger strikes her.

I think the executive chef was smart to coat his marshmallows in chocolate—it disguises their unpleasant green color. You still couldn't pay me to eat one of them, though. But the passengers seem to love them and the kitchen can barely keep up with demand.

Olivia is sitting at the table where Hamish and I used to have our Scrabble matches. Seeing her there makes me wonder what the Scotsman is up to now. After making his escape from the hotel bathroom at the Scrabble tournament, he hasn't been seen since. There were reports that he had turned up in the Maldives, but those turned out to be false.

How do I know all this? Well, I did something cringe-worthy this afternoon. I phoned the German restaurant that Erich took me to in Amsterdam. When a woman answered the phone, I panicked. What was I thinking—that Erich would answer the phone himself?

"Hello," the woman had barked into the phone again. "Is anyone there?"

I pretended I was calling to place a takeout order, then hemmed and hawed.

"I don't have all day," she said. "What do you want to order?"

I said the first thing that popped into my head.

"Could I have some pfälzer saumagen, please?"

"Hmm, pfälzer saumagen," the woman said dryly. "But I thought you didn't eat organ meat, Isabelle."

Feeling like a prank phone caller who's been caught out, I asked tentatively, "Is that you, Aunt C?"

"Of course it is, you silly girl," she snapped. "Who else did you think would answer the phone?"

"I think I dialed you by mistake," I said, wondering if running to the restroom and flushing my phone down the toilet would be a good idea. Anything to make this call end.

"Considering this number is classified, that seems highly unlikely." Aunt C let out an exasperated sigh. "Did Erich give it to you?"

I stalled, not wanting to get Erich in trouble. "Well, you see . . ."

"Just answer the question."

"Yes, he gave it to me," I confessed. "But it was only in case there was an emergency."

"And is this an emergency?" she asked.

I paced back and forth in my cabin, not sure how to answer. I eventually responded. The high-pitched squeak in my voice made me cringe. "I guess it depends on your definition of an emergency."

For some reason, this made Aunt C chuckle. Then she took pity on me, filling me in on Hamish's vanishing act and Erich's new partner. By the time the call was finished, I felt sick to my stomach, not just because Erich was working with some other woman, but because Aunt C hinted at concerns over my replacement's abilities.

While I'm obsessing over Erich and his new fake-fiancée, Olivia waves me over. I resolve to stop thinking about anything related to Erich. How long do we think this particular resolution will last?

"See that guy at the bar? The one with the red hair?" Olivia asks as I sit down. "He keeps trying to hit on me. I've told him repeatedly that I'm not interested, but the message doesn't seem to be getting through."

When I glance over at the bar, the redheaded man raises his glass at Olivia. She frowns. "Switch places with me, will you?"

Once she's seated with her back to her would-be suitor, I ask, "Did you tell him you have a boyfriend?"

"I shouldn't need to mention a boyfriend. If you tell a guy that you're not interested, that should be enough. There shouldn't have to be another man in the picture to get him to back off." She takes a sip of her wine, then adds, "Besides, I'm not sure if I have a boyfriend anymore."

"Your aunt mentioned something about his mother. What's going on?"

"Did you ever see *My Big Fat Greek Wedding*? This is kind of like that, but without the wedding. Definitely not the wedding." Olivia stares vacantly out the window. "Xander's mother always envisioned her son marrying a Greek woman. She's constantly playing matchmaker, bringing different girls to his taverna all the time."

"Even when you're there?" I ask.

"Yep. My presence doesn't stop her at all. An American woman, especially one who doesn't even have Greek ancestry, is not what she had planned for her son." Olivia leans forward. "I went to all this trouble of learning how to make her favorite dish, but she spent the entire meal pointing out what I did wrong."

"That sounds awful," I say. "What did Xander do?"

"He had a big argument with his mom, but it was in Greek, so I don't know what was said." Her eyes well up. "Afterward, he pretended like nothing was wrong, but he became so distant."

I make sympathetic noises, and she wipes away a tear. "Anyway, that's when Aunt Celeste suggested this cruise. She thought it would be good for me to get some time away from Xander."

"He'll realize what he's missing," I say, squeezing her hand. "Absence makes the heart grow fonder."

"But it's not just him. It's like I'm also dating his family," she says. "Have you ever been in that situation?"

I shake my head. My problems with Erich have nothing to do with his family. In some ways, family might be an easier issue to deal with. You know what you're up against. Everything is out in the open. But with Erich, it's the secrets that are keeping us apart.

Our conversation drifts off as Celeste sings "Bali Ha'i." Her voice is low and husky and she sways slowly in time to the music.

Olivia smiles. "When she was younger, my aunt was in an off-Broadway production of *South Pacific*. It's good to see her so happy. It was hard for her when Uncle Ernie passed away."

We listen to Celeste sing for a while. When she finishes, Olivia turns to me. "I love that song. A mysterious island calling to you to come to it—it's so romantic."

I furrow my brow. "Romantic? How so?"

"Did you ever meet someone you fell in love with right away, before you even knew that much about them? That's what it reminds me of—falling for a mysterious stranger and taking a chance on love." She blushes, then toys with her wineglass. "I know, I'm being silly. You can't fall in love with someone you know nothing about, right?"

I nod in agreement, but honestly, I'm wondering if she's wrong. Is it possible that I'm in love with Erich, a man I know nothing about?

* * *

"What are you two girls talking about?" Celeste sits at the table and a waiter instantly rushes up with a bottle of champagne for her.

As he pours her a glass, he asks what else he can do

to make her stay aboard the *Abenteuer* more enjoyable. "Anything you want, madame, it is yours."

"Well, there was this tattoo I was thinking of getting," Celeste says. "But I keep changing my mind about the design."

The waiter looks flummoxed. This is probably the first time a passenger has asked his opinion on what kind of tattoo to get. "What are you considering?" he asks.

"I was originally thinking of something that says, 'Floss.' Dental hygiene is important, don't you think?"

The waiter unconsciously runs his tongue across his front teeth, and I realize I've done the same thing. Funny how a mere mention of flossing can make you worry that you have something stuck between your teeth.

"Yes, dental hygiene is important, madame," he says.

Celeste takes a sip of her champagne. "Lately, I've been thinking of getting a tattoo of a cat."

The waiter smiles. Probably thinking—crazy cat lady, I've seen this kind before. "Yes, a kitten tattoo would be nice. Perhaps a calico or Siamese?"

She waves a hand in the air. "No, not that kind of cat. I was thinking about one of those scanning devices."

Olivia furrows her brow. "Do you mean a CAT scan?" She turns to me. "My dad was just telling us about the CAT scan he had done. I bet that's what put it in her head."

"Yes, that's it." Celeste turns back to the waiter. "Don't you think that would make a nice tattoo?"

He shifts the bottle of champagne from one arm to another. "Um . . ."

Olivia pats her aunt's arm. "We should let him get back to work, don't you think?"

"Of course," Celeste says. "But first, can you get Olivia and Isabelle some champagne glasses? Bubbles are meant to be shared."

The waiter shoots me a look. The champagne is reserved for passengers, not the staff. Especially the premium stuff he's serving Celeste. Not wanting to ruffle feathers, I ask for a glass of sparkling water instead.

"Are you sure, dear?" Celeste asks. "After that wonderful welcome presentation of yours, you deserve to celebrate."

"Water's fine," I say.

As the waiter rushes off to put in the order, Celeste looks at me. "Now, time to tell me about this mystery man of yours. What does he look like? Any birthmarks? What does he do for a living? Does he like chocolate? What's his star sign? What movie can you see him starring in?"

Celeste's random string of questions makes me smile. I answer the easy ones first. "He has blond hair and blue eyes. From what I've seen, he doesn't have any birthmarks."

"From what you've seen?" Celeste arches an eyebrow. "We'll come back to that later."

My face flushes as I remember how Erich opened the door to his cabin wearing nothing but a towel. Trying to distract myself, I plow on with answering Celeste's question. "Um, I think he likes chocolate. Doesn't everyone? I can totally see him as James Bond."

"Ooh, James Bond," Olivia says. "Sounds like he's dangerous and sexy."

I groan. That James Bond answer slipped out so naturally, but the last thing I need is for anyone to have the slightest reason to connect Erich with secret spies.

"Did I say James Bond? I meant James T. Kirk."

"From *Star Trek*?" Olivia asks.

"Yeah, that's the one," I say, feigning a confidence that I don't have. Maybe it's *Star Trek*. Maybe it's *Star Wars*. I always get them mixed up.

"Anyway, he's a pharmaceutical sales representative. . ." My voice trails off as the waiter serves Olivia and me our drinks. I don't want him to hear me talk about Erich. Half the crew still believes I had an affair with him. When the waiter leaves, I say, "Erich says it's a pretty boring job. About as far away from a secret spy as you can get."

"If you say so, dear." Celeste leans forward, her eyes sparkling. "Now, let's get to the heart of the matter. Last time I heard from you, you were head-over-heels for this guy."

I cock my head to one side. "I was?"

"You might not have said that explicitly," Celeste admits. "I could tell that's how you felt though. But something happened. What was it?"

"It wasn't meant to be, that's all." Then I try to change the subject. "I'd love to hear about your days performing off-Broadway."

Celeste sees right through me. "Another time, dear. Now, there are four major reasons why relationships don't work. Different backgrounds. That's a barrier that can be overcome. It's not always easy, but it can be done. You said that your fellow is German. Could that be the issue?"

Not waiting for me to answer, she shakes her head. "No, that's not it. Then there's betrayal. That can be hard to move past as well. But that's not the problem either, is it?"

"No," I say, wishing this conversation was over.

Olivia pipes up. "Okay, so if it's not betrayal or different backgrounds, what is it?"

Celeste looks at me thoughtfully. "It's a matter of trust. Isabelle doesn't know if she can trust him."

I avert my eyes and study my water glass. "Erich is a consummate professional. I'd trust him with my life."

"How often to you put your life on the line with a pharmaceutical sales representative?" Olivia asks.

I bite back a smile. If only she knew what Erich

really did for a living.

"You don't trust him personally," Celeste says. "Is that it?"

"Trust is predicated on being completely open with one another, don't you think?" I ask.

"Ah, he's the secretive type." Celeste's smile fades. "The very first man I fell in love with was the same way. He was evasive about what he did for a living. For a while I thought he was an insurance agent, but when I found out what he really did, well . . ."

Olivia leans forward. "I didn't know there was anyone before Uncle Ernie. What happened?"

"He broke up with me. I was devastated at first. But it was for the best." She pats Olivia's hand. "And then I met your uncle. The most wonderful man in the world."

"Did you ever wonder what happened to that first guy?" I ask.

"Sometimes. But, we're talking about you, remember?" She motions at me. "Go on."

"I understand why Erich's secretive," I say. "It's critical in his line of work."

"I can see that," Olivia says. "The pharmaceutical industry is cut-throat. Companies don't want their competitors to steal their trade secrets. But he's keeping other secrets from you, is that it?"

I shrug. "It doesn't really matter. The chances of our paths crossing again are next to nothing."

"Sometimes, it's easier to make a fresh start,"

Olivia says. "Love shouldn't be this hard."

"Don't make any hasty decisions, dear," Celeste says to her niece. Then she turns to me. "And you shouldn't write your fellow off so easily, either. After all, you have secrets of your own, don't you? Maybe the two of you are destined to become each other's secret-keepers."

"Secret-keepers," I say softly to myself. That has a nice ring to it.

Celeste fights back a yawn. "Well, girls, it's bedtime for this old broad."

As we say goodnight, I remember something. "You said there were four reasons why relationships didn't work out, but you only mentioned three. What was the fourth?"

"Oh, that one can be a real deal-breaker," Celeste says. "Watch out if one of you is a cat person and the other one is a dog person."

* * *

It's been fun having Celeste and Olivia aboard. They've been a great distraction. Between keeping busy with work, then spending time with the two of them when I'm not on duty, I've managed to stop thinking about Erich.

Okay, that's a lie. I have dark circles under my eyes because I can't sleep. I've tried everything—counting sheep, listening to a meditation app, even avoiding caffeine—but nothing works. Memories of Erich play through my head until the early hours of the morning.

But the time with them has flown by and now it's the night before we dock in Basel. The night before Erich undertakes the mission with my replacement.

Celeste, Olivia, and I are sitting on the sun deck, not far from the spot where Erich and I had that amazing kiss. Celeste is leafing through a travel magazine while Olivia texts someone. From the expression on her face, I think it's Xander.

"There's a piece in there about this riverboat," I tell Celeste. "There's even a picture of me playing Scrabble."

She flips to the article, then smiles. "Don't you look pretty with your hair down. Why don't you wear it that way more often?"

"The bun is regulation." I adjust one of the hairpins so it isn't jabbing into my scalp. "I could cut my hair short so that I don't have to tie it back, but I don't really want to do that. I only have a few more months left working aboard the boat, so I'm trying to put up with it."

Celeste nods, then looks back at the magazine. Then she gasps, causing Olivia and I both to stare at her.

"Is that who I think it is?" Celeste pulls a pair of reading glasses out of her purse and examines the magazine more closely. Then she points at one of the pictures. "Who's that man there?" she asks me. "The one in the background. Do you remember his name?"

"Oh, that's Hamish MacDougall," I say. "He was my Scrabble partner."

Celeste looks ashen. Her hands are shaking and she nearly drops the magazine.

"What is it, Aunt Celeste?" Olivia asks. "What's wrong?"

"It's nothing. I thought I recognized someone, but I was mistaken." Celeste hands me the magazine, then stands. "I think I'm going to turn in. I'll see you girls in the morning."

As she walks away, Olivia turns to me. "What do you think that was about?"

"I don't know," I say. "Something spooked her."

"I've never seen her react that way before," Olivia says. "I better go check on her."

She gives me a quick hug, then rushes after her aunt. I flip through the magazine, trying to figure out what it was that made Celeste leave so abruptly. Something nags me at the back of my brain that I can't put my finger on. Something about my friend Ginny.

Then it hits me. When Ginny went to visit Celeste in Greece, Celeste told her about the first man she fell in love with. It was the same story that Celeste had told Olivia and I earlier, but with one critical difference. The reason she broke up with her first love is because she couldn't accept his career choice, so to speak. A career that involved stealing jewelry.

I turn to the article that Zoe wrote and look at the picture Celeste had been examining. Is it possible that the jewel thief Celeste used to be in love with is the very same man as Hamish MacDougall?

CHAPTER 14
A SURPRISE DELIVERY

When we dock in Basel the next morning, I say a teary goodbye to Celeste and Olivia. They're both heading back to Greece. Celeste has decided to spend what's left of the summer at her villa there, and Olivia is going to see if she can work things out with Xander. I try to talk to Celeste about Hamish before she leaves, but she clams up.

Celeste envelops me in a hug. "I have a feeling things are about to take a mysterious turn for you, Isabelle," she says. "Stay in touch, dear, and let me know what happens."

After they leave, I go back to helping Sophia with checkout.

"Do you think your friend was the undercover passenger?" Sophia asks once we say goodbye to the final passenger. "If so, I hope she gives us a good report to Head Office."

"I don't think she was," I say. "She did leave a glowing review on social media though."

"I guess that's something." Sophia sighs. "But that means we're still on pins and needles wondering who the undercover passenger is."

While we're filling out paperwork, a man walks into the reception area bearing a large paper bag.

"Sorry, sir," Sophia says. "We don't begin boarding for another four hours."

"I have a delivery for Isabelle Martinez," he says.

Sophia points at me, and he deposits the bag on the counter.

"What's this?" I ask.

He shrugs. "I don't get paid to ask questions."

I open it up and pull out a Styrofoam container. My jaw drops when I see what's inside. "Pfälzer saumagen? What the heck?"

Sophia peers over my shoulder. "You got lunch?"

"Hey, wait a minute," I yell after the deliveryman as he's walking out the door. "Where did you get this?"

"I picked it up at the airport," he says over his shoulder. "It came on a private plane from Amsterdam."

Before I can rush after him to ask him more questions, Frau Albrecht marches into the reception area and glares at me. "How many times do I have to tell you—no eating while on duty."

"But I'm not eating," I say. "I didn't even order this."

She snorts and picks up the paper bag. "It says Isabelle Martinez right here."

"But—"

Frau Albrecht holds up her hand. "Eat on your own time. Now, if you need me, I'll be inspecting the cabins." As she sets the bag back on the counter, a card falls out.

Sophia picks it up and discretely hands it to me. Once the older woman leaves, I open it up. When I read what it says, I'm in even more shock.

The organization needs you. Our mutual acquaintance has grave concerns about your replacement's ability to carry out the task in question. He refuses to ask you to help, so I'm forced to do so on his behalf. It's not too late to reconsider your decision. Without you, lives could be in jeopardy.

PS Enjoy the pfälzer saumagen. Our mutual acquaintance told me about the time he introduced you to it.

As I tuck the card back into the envelope, I notice my hands are shaking. It's obvious who the note is from—Aunt C. She must have had the food flown from her restaurant in Amsterdam to Basel. And the "mutual acquaintance" she refers to is obviously Erich. I can't believe he told Aunt C about the time he ordered me a dish in Mainz made with organ meat, a dish I ended up enjoying.

This is blackmail in its most blatant form. If I don't help Erich, then the unthinkable could happen.

"You look white as a ghost. Is it bad news?" Sophia asks.

"It's the worst kind of news," I say. "The kind that means you have to do something that terrifies you in order to help someone you love."

* * *

Yes, that's right. I said the L-word out loud. This isn't something theoretical anymore. I love Erich. I might not know any details about his background, I may not know what shaped him into the man he is today, but I know the essence of him. And that's what I love—the part of him that's true yesterday, today, and tomorrow.

Okay, that's enough cheesiness, Isabelle. You've got a party to get to.

"Remember Erich Zimmermann?" I ask Sophia.

"The hot VIP from Germany? Sure," Sophia says while she prints out the list of passengers who will be boarding the boat later today. She glances down at my legs. "That rash cream he gave you did wonders."

"It was actually the nylons," I say. "Once Frau Albrecht told me I didn't have to wear them anymore, the rash cleared up."

"That was Head Office's doing," Sophia says. "Frau Albrecht was furious that she had to make so many exceptions for you. I just wish they'd make an exception for me."

"What do you mean?"

Sophia sets the stack of papers to one side. "I'm dying to tell someone. Can you keep a secret?"

"Of course." If only Sophia knew how good I am at keeping secrets.

Sophia looks around to make sure we won't be overheard, then whispers, "Auguste Renoir proposed."

"Oh, my gosh, that's wonderful." I give her a hug, then say, "Let me see the ring."

Sophia pulls a delicate gold chain out of her blouse. Dangling from it is a gorgeous diamond ring.

"That's stunning," I tell her. "But why aren't you wearing it on your hand?"

She frowns as she slips the necklace back inside her blouse. "Employees aren't allowed to date. If we want to be together, one of us is going to have to resign. Since Auguste has a more senior role, it makes sense for me to find another job."

"But if he stays aboard the *Abenteuer*, that would mean the two of you wouldn't see each other very often," I say.

"I know. He's offered to quit, but I told him no. He has good career prospects with the cruise line." Sophia wipes away a tear, then plasters on her usual smile. "Anyway, enough of that."

"But you and Auguste . . . I wish there was something I could do."

"Do you mind if we don't talk about it anymore?" Sophia adjusts the collar of her blouse. "Now, why did you mention Herr Zimmermann?"

"Well, you were right in a way about us," I say.

She claps her hands together. "I knew it. The two of you were having an affair."

"No, we weren't," I say. "Well, we kissed once, but that was it."

"Uh-huh." She looks dubious. "So what happened?"

"We decided that a relationship wasn't workable."

"But he's not a passenger anymore," Sophia points out. "The two of you can date now."

"That's what I wanted to talk to you about. He's here in Basel. I have a chance to see him, but I'm on duty tonight. I'm supposed to give the welcome presentation."

Sophia smiles. "Go on. I'll cover for you."

"Are you sure?"

"I'll tell Frau Albrecht that you're sick. Just make sure you're back here by tomorrow morning when we set sail."

After thanking her a million times, I rush to my cabin to grab everything I'll need for this mission. As I pack the evening gown Erich had arranged for me to wear to the party, I make a mental note to see if he can pull one last string with Head Office and get an exception made for Sophia.

* * *

I'm standing outside Erich's hotel suite, but can't bring myself to knock on the door. What am I supposed to say when he answers? It's not like I'm going to tell him that I love him. I barely admitted that to myself. The last thing I'm going to do is confess that to him.

After stalling for a few minutes, I finally summon up the courage and rap on the door. Steeling myself for an awkward encounter with Erich, I clasp my hands in front of me and try to project an air of confidence.

When the door opens, I'm confronted with something I should have anticipated if I had been thinking clearly—a gorgeous woman wearing a stunning black beaded evening gown. Of course, Erich's new partner would be here in his suite. She's posing as Svetlana, the fake fiancée.

The woman greets me in Russian, and, even though I understand what she's saying, I stand there with my jaw open, unable to speak.

She repeats her greeting in German, French, English, and even Cantonese. I finally manage to respond, saying, "Room service."

She arches an eyebrow, taking in my obvious lack

of hotel uniform and tray.

"Who is it?" a man calls out in Russian.

My heart flutters at the sound of Erich's voice. Feeling like I might collapse any minute, I brace myself against the doorjamb.

"A woman talking nonsense. I think she is drunk."

I jab a finger in Fake Svetlana's direction. "I'm not drunk. I'm just . . ." My voice trails off when Erich walks up behind her.

"Isabelle?" he asks. Then he smiles at me. The hugest smile I've ever seen on him. One that lights up his eyes. "What are you doing here?"

"You know this woman?" Fake Svetlana shoots me a look that sends shivers down my spine. She could rival Aunt C in the intimidation department.

Before Erich can answer, his phone rings. He puts it to his ear, and his expression sobers. He listens for a few moments, then hands it to Fake Svetlana.

After a one-way conversation, she thrusts the phone back at Erich and glares at him. "That was Aunt C. She says that I've been replaced." She turns her icy stare in my direction. "Replaced by her."

Every word she utters is dripping with venom and I take a few steps back. I look around the hallway for the security cameras. Ah, there's one, right across from Erich's hotel suite. Aunt C must have tapped into it. That's the only explanation for how she knew I was standing at Erich's door at this very moment.

"Well, perhaps that's for the best," Erich says

placidly.

"The best?" She spins around and grabs Erich by his arms. "I'll tell you what's for the best. And it's not this—"

Erich's phone rings again. He looks in the direction of the security camera and nods. Then he hands the phone to Fake Svetlana without answering it. "I think it's for you."

As she listens to the person on the other end of the line, I stare at the carpet wishing this awkward moment would be over. Fake Svetlana has basically been fired because I showed up. There are some weird parallels with how Maria, the original tour manager aboard the *Abenteuer*, was replaced by me. And now this woman.

The phone call over, Fake Svetlana storms past Erich into the suite. Erich sighs, then motions for me to follow him inside. While I wait in the living room, I listen to Fake Svetlana yell at Erich. The woman has an impressive knowledge of Russian curse words.

She flounces back out, a wheeled suitcase in tow behind her. As she barrels past me toward the door, she jams her elbow into my side. "Sorry," she says sarcastically.

"Wait," Erich calls out.

Fake Svetlana spins around, a hopeful look on her face. "Have you changed your mind?"

Erich shakes his head, then points at her hand. "I need the ring back."

She pulls it off her finger and flings it at him. He makes an impressive catch, and I wonder if he played baseball as a kid.

After the door slams behind her, Erich turns to me. "Sorry, you had to go through that."

"She's kind of scary," I say, half-joking, half-not. "Were you worried she might knife you in your sleep?"

"That was the least of my worries," he says. "She wasn't up to the mission. I was fearful she would get us killed."

"Aunt C said you had grave concerns about her."

"She wasn't supposed to tell you that." Erich takes my hands in his and squeezes them. "I told her not to drag you into this."

"It was my decision," I say firmly. "I'm ready to face my fears. The mission is a go."

We talk for a few minutes, and I finally convince Erich that I'm up for it.

"If you're absolutely sure," he says holding up engagement ring. "Then would you do the honor of being my fake fiancée again?"

I grin as he slips the ring on my finger. It feels good to be back working with Erich. Whether we have a future as anything more . . . well, I can't think about that now. I need to focus on the mission.

CHAPTER 15
HAMSTER BRUSHES

As we walk up the marble stairs to the entrance of the historic mansion where the party is taking place, Erich turns to me and says, "You look gorgeous."

"It's the dress," I say, running my hands down the silver sequined evening gown I'm wearing. "Anyone would look good in this."

"It's not the dress. It's you," he says. "You'd look good in a sack of potatoes."

"Please don't talk about potatoes. I haven't had any for ages."

"But after you pulled out of the mission, didn't you start eating them again?"

"No, I didn't. I don't know why. Maybe some part of me knew that I would end up playing the role of a Russian woman with a potato allergy after all?"

Erich points at the charm bracelet on my wrist. "You better let me hang onto that. Scrabble isn't really the real Svetlana's thing." He helps me unclasp it, then slips it in his pocket.

When we walk into the grand ballroom, the sheikh greets us. He extends his hand to Erich. "I'm honored that you would break your self-imposed exile to attend this event, Mr. Petrov."

My eyes widen slightly at the use of the Russian name. Then I check myself. Tonight, we're not Erich and Isabelle. We're Andrei Petrov and Svetlana Sidirov. Two eccentric Russian recluses. One a billionaire who made his fortune in potato peelers and the other, his fiancée, a famous hamster groomer.

Potato peelers and hamster groomers. That sounds absurd, doesn't it? If I hadn't personally seen the files on Andrei and Svetlana, I'd think it was a joke. But, nope, they're real people.

Erich clasps the sheikh's shoulder. "For a deal this important, I felt I had no choice. I built my company from the ground up. I can't sell it without looking the buyer directly in the eye."

"There is wisdom in this," the sheikh says. "My father always said that there is no substitute for conducting business face-to-face."

Erich puts his arm around my shoulders. "May I introduce my fiancée?"

"Miss Sidirov, what a delightful pleasure," the sheikh says. "My daughter will be thrilled to hear that

I met you. She has one of those longhaired hamsters. What are they called?"

"An Angora?" I ask.

"Yes, that is the breed. But its fur is constantly getting tangled and matted. What would you suggest?"

"Well, I'm introducing a new line of hamster brushes. Each one is carved from organic ebony and the bristles are handcrafted by Tibetan monks. They're guaranteed to keep your hamster's hair silky smooth and free of tangles."

The sheikh nods slowly, then summons one of his assistants over. When he has an intense conversation with him in Arabic, Erich shoots me a warning look. I twist my fake engagement ring around my finger. Was the bit about the hamster brushes over the top? Have I blown our cover already?

"I will buy two hundred of them," the sheikh says to me. "I have instructed my assistant to place the order."

I breathe a sigh of relief. We make some more small talk about hamster wheels, then the sheikh excuses himself so that he can greet some new arrivals.

"Hamster brushes?" Erich whispers to me. "Where did that come from?"

"I don't know. It popped into my head. I got nervous, and I improvised." I grip Erich's hand. "Oh, my gosh, the minute the assistant tries to place the order on Svetlana's website, he's going to realize that I'm a fraud. She doesn't sell hamster brushes."

"She does now," Erich says, tapping out a text on his phone. "I've got our IT department on it. They'll create a cloned version of her site, making sure hamster brushes are featured prominently."

"Right, your IT department," I say dryly. "The same ones whose systems failed during the Scrabble tournament? We're trusting those guys?"

"Aunt C has made some organizational changes," Erich says. "I'm sure it will be fine."

He sounds confident, but from the way his brow is furrowed, I think he's worried.

"Okay, let's focus on what we can control," I say. "What does the point person for the Nouveau Rouge Order look like?"

"All we know is that it's a woman and that she'll be wearing a red dress and a cat brooch," Erich says.

"Why a cat brooch?"

"Our intel wasn't that specific."

A waiter passes by with a tray of hors d'oeuvres. I snake out a hand to snag a potato puff, but Erich stops me. He grabs my hand and raises it to his lips. "Remember, you're allergic to potatoes," he says before kissing the back of my hand.

"So that's all you have to go on—red dress and a cat brooch," I say, trying to ignore the sensation of his lips on my skin.

"Our source didn't want to give too much away," Erich says.

"Well, they definitely succeeded." As another waiter presents us with a tantalizing display of food, I sigh. "Why is everything made out of potatoes?"

"I suspect it's in celebration of my business deal with the sheikh." Erich motions for the waiter to move on to the next group of guests. "I promise that when this mission is over, I'll get you the biggest baked potato you've ever seen."

"I'll hold you to that." Then I point toward the other side of the room. "Look at that woman talking with the sheikh. She's wearing a red dress."

"There are a number of women wearing red tonight. We need her to turn around so that we can see if she has a cat brooch. Once we confirm that it's her, we'll execute the plan." Erich strokes his fake beard and looks at me thoughtfully. "Are you absolutely sure you're okay with going through with this?"

I pull his hand away from his chin. "Be careful with that. It looks like it might come off."

"You didn't answer my question."

"I'm absolutely, one hundred percent certain that I'm okay to go through with this," I say, emphasizing every word. "The plan is straightforward. We go to the office. You hoist me up to an air-conditioning vent. I climb through the ductwork until I get to the library. Then I turn this sparkly ring into a recording device, capture everything that's said, make my way back to the office, and presto—we've captured ourselves some terrorists. What could possibly go wrong?"

"She's turning around." Erich tugs on my arm.

I look at the woman's dress. "There's the cat brooch. The target has been identified and confirmed." Then my gaze travels upward and I see her face. "You've got to be kidding me."

"What is it?" Erich asks.

"That's Bob," I say.

"Bob from the Scrabble tournament?" Erich squints in the woman's direction. "Are you sure?"

"Positive." Then I pull Erich toward me and plant a kiss on his lips.

* * *

"What was that for?" Erich asks.

"Shush." I shift our position slightly so that Erich's back is facing Bob. Burrowing my head into Erich's chest so that I'm hidden from view, I whisper, "I don't want Bob to see us."

"And kissing creates an invisibility cloak?" Erich asks in an undertone.

"I was afraid you would say something too loudly and draw attention to us."

"Uh-huh." Erich twists his head and looks behind

him. "She's turned back around. Let's make a break for it."

We move quickly through the ballroom, keeping clusters of other guests between us and Bob. Once we're in the clear, we dash to the office. I ask Erich why Bob is here. "I thought Bob was a fence, but if she's here, that means she's also a member of the Nouveau Rouge Order."

Erich closes and locks the office door, then turns to face me. "It's possible that our intel was faulty."

"IT problems, faulty intel—does anything in the organization work?" I ask.

"Aunt C makes a mean apple strudel. And we do have an excellent dental plan." After reaching up and removing the grating from the ceiling, he glances back at me. "Ready?"

"Just a sec." I slip off my heels, then detach the skirt from my dress, revealing a pair of form-fitting shorts. They're covered in silver sequins, like my dress, but far more practical for crawling through ductwork.

Erich whistles. "You're the sexiest hamster groomer I've ever worked with."

"Enough staring at my legs, mister. Hoist me up."

Once I'm inside the air-conditioning duct, I hear Erich's voice in my ear. "Testing, testing."

"You're coming in loud and clear. I hope you can hear me because my mike is sewn into the neckline of my dress, and adjusting it would be a challenge," I say. "It's more cramped in here than it was in the cardboard boxes."

"You're fine," Erich says. "Remember not to speak unless you absolutely have to. Sound carries through this ducting."

"It's pitch-black up here," I say. "You're going to tell me when to turn left and right, correct?"

"Yes, don't worry. There's an app on my phone with a map of the ductwork. Your position is overlaid on it. I'll be tracking you the entire time." He pauses for a beat, then says, "Are you sure you're okay?"

Actually, I'm not okay. My heart is racing and my skin is clammy. But I can't tell Erich that or he'll call a halt to the mission. So I lie. "Couldn't be better."

"Okay, the sheikh starts his meetings promptly. That means you only have four minutes to get to the library." Erich gulps audibly. "Forward seven feet, then right."

I inch through the ductwork while he calls out directions, banging my head a few times, and scraping my knees on the sharp corners.

"Three minutes, twenty-two seconds remaining," Erich says. He continues guiding me through the ductwork, then finally says, "One more left turn and you should be there."

As I round the corner, I see light ahead. That must be coming through the grating in the library. Erich confirms that I'm in position. "Time to turn on the recorder," he says. "Once the meeting is finished, and the library is clear, I'll guide you back to the office."

I press the hidden latch on the engagement ring and the diamond pops open, revealing the high-tech equipment inside. According to Erich, this thing is capable of picking up even the faintest of conversations.

When the door to the library opens, I suck in my breath. Peering through the vent, I watch as Bob enters the room, followed by the sheikh. He offers her a drink, but she refuses.

"Let's get down to business," she says in a clipped British accent.

"As you wish," the sheikh says. "Let me see the necklace."

Bob hitches up her skirt. Strapped to one of her legs is a gun, and on the other is a small velvet bag. The sheikh eyes her cautiously, then relaxes when she removes the bag and presents it to him.

"Ah, it's even more beautiful in person." The sheikh holds up the necklace and the diamonds and emeralds sparkle in the light from the chandelier. Then he examines it more closely using a jeweler's loupe.

"Satisfactory?" Bob asks.

The sheikh slips the necklace back into the bag. "Yes, I'm satisfied."

"Excellent," Bob says. "Now the location of the weapons."

While the sheikh reels off a set of coordinates, I

feel something crawling on my right leg. Something cold and slimy. What kinds of creatures live in air-conditioning ducts? It continues up my leg and when it reaches the bottom of my shorts and bites me, I yelp.

Bob looks directly at the vent. Then she grabs the necklace back from the sheikh. "You set me up."

The sheikh holds his hands up. "I didn't. I swear."

"Liar," Bob shrieks.

I don't wait to see what happens next, inching backward as fast as I can. The creature isn't crawling on my leg anymore. That's because it's now in my hair. I've seen this exact same scenario in a horror movie. It didn't end well for the heroine.

"Erich," I hiss. "I need directions."

There's no response. Of course, there isn't. This is the perfect timing for another technology snafu. Yes, that's sarcasm. Do you know how hard it is to crawl backwards through ductwork, especially when it's shaped like a rat maze? Add in the slimy creature in my hair and it's no wonder I'm having an anxiety attack.

After a few wrong turns and dead-ends, I finally make it back to the office. I slip down through the vent, landing with a thud on my hands and knees. I shake my head vigorously. When something jumps out and slithers away, I shudder.

"Erich, where are you?" The mission has been

blown," I say as I get to my feet and turn around. "We need to . . ."

My voice trails off as I see who's in the room—Bob, and she's holding a gun to Erich's head.

"Fancy a game of Scrabble?" she asks me. Then she cracks Erich across his temple and he crumples to the floor.

CHAPTER 16
THE UNDERVALUED LETTER OPENER

I scream Erich's name, but before I can rush over to him, Bob waves her gun at me.

"Stay where you are," she says.

I clasp my hands behind my back and press the diamond back into position, then look around the room to get my bearings. In front of me is a large oak desk. File folders and pens are strewn across the top of the desk, but there's nothing I can use as a weapon. Off to the side are built-in bookshelves. Perhaps I could hurl one of those thick leather-bound encyclopedias at Bob and knock her off balance?

As I edge slowly in that direction, Bob aims her gun in my direction. "I told you to stay where you were. Let me see your hands."

I hold my hands in front of me. "See, they're empty."

"I bet you wish that was a real engagement ring, don't you?" She snorts, then kicks Erich's shoulder. "Hank told me that you were gaga over this one."

My jaw drops. "Hank? Hank Sinclair from Alabama? The guy who was on my first cruise?"

"The Nouveau Rouge Order is everywhere," Bob says. "I wanted one of my agents on board to keep an eye on Hamish. I needed that necklace to make a deal with the sheikh."

I'm having a hard time reconciling the woman in front of me with the woman I played Scrabble against in the tournament. This Bob has an elegant hairdo and is dressed in a chic evening gown. Her eyes are cold, and she handles the gun in her hand like a pro. The other Bob wore a tinfoil hat and pink mittens. She seemed harmless at the time, but now I know how deeply I was deceived.

"Hank is one of your agents?" I twist the engagement ring around my finger. "That would mean you're one of the Nouveau Rouge Order leaders."

"I'm *the* leader," she says, waving the gun around for emphasis.

"So she wasn't an ordinary fence," I mumble to myself. "I played Scrabble with the leader of the Nouveau Rouge Order and let her slip through my fingers."

"Speak up," Bob says. "I can't stand people who don't enunciate the words."

"I didn't say anything."

"You're lying. I hate people that lie to me." She takes a step toward me. "Do you want to know what happened to the last person who lied to me?"

"You mean the sheikh?"

Bob grabs me by the throat with one hand. "Of course, I mean the sheikh. You're even stupider than you look."

As I struggle to breathe, I cast my eyes across the room to where Erich is lying. Is this how it ends? Bob kills us both before I have a chance to tell Erich how I feel about him?

Then I see something glinting in the light of the desk lamp. What looks like a piece of metal is peeking out from underneath one of the file folders. I reach for it, grasping it with the tips of my fingers. As it slides out, I give a mental shout of triumph when I see that it's a letter opener.

When it comes to office supplies, I had always undervalued the run-of-the-mill letter opener. Honestly, how hard is it to rip an envelope open? But after tonight, I'm going to be singing the letter opener's praises because now it's going to double as a very effective weapon.

The look of surprise on Bob's face when I use the letter opener on her is priceless. But it doesn't compare to Erich's expression when he opens his eyes and sees Bob lying on the floor clutching her side.

* * *

Erich gets to his feet and retrieves the gun and the letter opener from the floor. He sets them on a table in the far corner of the room, then points at Bob. "Did you do this?"

"Forget about her," I say, rushing to his side. "Are you okay?"

"I'll be fine." Erich rubs his temple and winces. Then he hands me his phone. "Press the star key. That will connect you with headquarters. Tell them to send in the strike team."

While I tell headquarters what happened, as well as alert them to the fact that Hank is also a member of the terrorist group, Erich checks to make sure Bob's wounds aren't life-threatening. Using a throw from an armchair, he applies a makeshift bandage. Then he pulls some zip ties out of his pocket and secures her.

"There, that should hold her." The look he gives her is full of contempt, but when he turns his expression softens. "What about you? Are you okay?"

After reassuring him that I'm fine, I tell him that the strike team is on their way. I glance over at the door to the office. "You locked that. How did she get in here?"

Erich walks over to Bob and yanks the cat brooch off her dress. He turns it around and inspects the back. "Yep, thought as much. This is a multipurpose tool disguised as jewelry. There's a screwdriver, corkscrew, pliers, and even a lock pick. I should show this to the team back at headquarters."

He shoves it in his pocket, then pulls the charm bracelet out. "I almost forgot I had this in here."

The door swings open and two heavily armed agents rush into the room. "Everything okay, sir?" one of them asks.

"We're fine, thanks to Isabelle." Erich removes his wig, then pulls his fake beard off. "Where are we at with the sheikh?"

"We have him in custody. We're screening the rest of the guests to make sure no one affiliated with the sheikh or the Nouveau Rouge Order slips through." The agent looks at Bob. "After we make a final sweep through the mansion, we'll come back for this one."

Erich nods. "Any report from IT? My comms link with Isabelle went down. Do we know if they got the feed from the recorder?"

The agent rolls his eyes. "They're giving us their usual song and dance about restoring communications, but they assure us that the data is secure."

Erich sighs. "James Bond never has these issues."

"At least you have a good dental plan," I quip. "So what if you have a few computer glitches here and there."

The agents chuckle, then excuse themselves to

continue the sweep of the building.

I pull the fake engagement ring off my finger. "I suppose you'll be needing this back."

As I hand it to Erich, he mutters something. It sounds like he said, "Next time I give you a ring, it will be for real," but that's ridiculous, right? We have the head of a terrorist organization lying on the floor. Who could possibly be thinking about marriage at time like this?

Erich holds up the charm bracelet. "Do you want to keep this as a memento?"

I take the bracelet from his hand. "A memento? A souvenir of our time together. That sounds so final."

Bob groans. I glance over to make sure she hasn't bit through her zip ties. When I look back at Erich, his icy-blue eyes are glistening. Are those tears?

He clears his throat. "I don't want this to be final. We work well together. We're a very, um, efficient team."

"Oh," I say, suddenly deflated. "You're talking about our working relationship."

"No, that's not what I mean." He starts to run his fingers through his hair, then grimaces when he touches the side of his head where Bob struck him. "She did a number on me."

I close the gap between us, and hold out the bracelet. "Can you help me put this on?"

Erich takes the bracelet from me and nods. He strokes my wrist gently after he fastens the clasp, and we both start to speak at the same time.

"Ladies first," he says.

"I want you to be my secret-keeper," I say quietly. "I want you to know everything about me, not because you read it in a file, but because I told it to you."

I shiver as he trails his fingers down my neck. "Secret-keeper. I like the sound of that." His lips follow his fingers, lightly brushing the skin on my neck. "There's a secret I don't share with anyone . . . until now."

Erich pulls back and leans against the desk. He moves a pile of file folders to one side and pats the spot next to him. I sit by his side and listen as he tells me his story. It takes me a moment to realize that he's speaking English with an American accent, not the German one I had grown used to.

"You asked me once where I was from in Germany. I don't know if you noticed, but I avoided answering."

"Oh, I noticed," I say gently.

"The truth is that I grew up in Iowa." When I turn my head to look at him, he adds, "I was born in Germany, but my parents died in a car accident when I was a baby. I was sent to live with my great-aunt and great uncle in the States. They did their best bringing me up, but I always knew that I was a burden to them."

I squeeze his hand. "No, that can't be true."

"It is," he says simply. "They never had children of

their own, and to be saddled with an infant in their golden years was something they didn't sign up for. They always made sure my basic needs were provided for, but a child need something more."

"A child needs love," I say.

Erich takes a deep breath, then continues. "I graduated high school at sixteen, then ran off to Europe. At first, I traveled around, but eventually found myself in Germany where I went to college. The other students were friendly, but I was a loner, preferring to keep my distance . . ."

Erich's voice trails off, and I scoot closer to him. He puts his arm around my shoulders and I lean into him. "Go on."

"Well, after college, I joined the organization—you know that part. It was great at first. Smart people, committed people, people who believed in something. I worked my way up through the ranks. Can you believe my first assignment was to the IT department?"

"Sounds like they've gone downhill ever since you left," I say.

He briefly chuckles, then turns more serious. "I was eventually assigned to work as a field agent. My partner was an experienced agent. She showed me the ropes. There isn't anything that woman didn't know about creating a convincing cover story. She was a pretty special lady."

"Was?" I ask.

Erich gets up and paces back and forth, pausing briefly to check on Bob's restraints. "She died during an operation."

"Oh, I'm sorry," I say, knowing how inadequate those words are. After a beat, I venture a guess. "Was she more than a colleague?"

"Yes." Erich sits back on the desk, and puts his head in his hands for a moment, then looks directly at me. "When she was killed, I swore that I'd never get close to anyone again. Especially not someone I work with. My feelings for her distracted me." Erich's voice cracks slightly. He clenches his fists, then slowly relaxes them. "If I had been more focused on the mission, maybe I could have prevented her death."

I want to reassure Erich that he's wrong, but I can't. Because I've experienced something so similar, that it's eerie. The only thing I can think to do is share my own secret.

"You know much of this already from my file," I say. "When I was in the Air Force, I worked as an intelligence analyst, which you know. Toward the end of my term of service I became involved in a relationship with a foreign officer. He was a member of an ally nation's defense forces on special assignment to our unit. I was so head over heels in love, that I wasn't focused on my work and I missed something . . . something important."

Erich leans over. "Hey, I already know all of this, and it wasn't your fault. A lot of people missed something that day."

"But if I hadn't been so caught up in daydreaming about this guy, I wouldn't have missed it. I was good at my job."

"I know that too," Erich says. "Why else do you think the organization wanted you for this mission?"

I chew on my lip for a moment. "There's more, though. Something that's not in the file you've seen. Something that only a few people know. The officer I fell in love with . . . he was a double agent. An operative for a hostile nation, and I didn't recognize the signs. If I had, maybe he could have been stopped. But I didn't, and I can't even begin to tell you how badly he compromised our systems."

I look sideways at Erich. He looks stunned, but after a moment he takes my hand and kisses the back of it.

"Thank you for trusting me with your secret," he says. "For the record, I doubt if you would have known if he was a double agent or not. But I can see how you feel like you should have."

"That's why this has been so hard for me," I say. "Never quite knowing if someone is who or what they say they are. That's when the anxiety attacks began. When my term of service was up, I walked away from the Air Force and straight into a glamorous career at the mini-mart. I became a shell of my original self."

"But you're not that woman anymore," Erich says. "You're strong, determined, and smart."

"Just like my grandmother," I say, glancing down at the ring of hers on my right hand. I look back at Erich. "I have one last secret to share with you."

Erich smiles. "Me too."

"Gentlemen first this time."

Erich cups my face with his hands. "I love you, Isabelle. And I can't imagine a future without you, my secret-keeper."

"You stole my secret," I say.

"You mean you . . ." His voice trails off, waiting for me to finish the sentence.

"Yes, I love you too, Erich," I say as he leans down to kiss me. Then I realize I have one more important question, and I pull back. "Is your name even Erich or is that a cover?"

Erich grins. "Funnily enough, Erich is my real name. For some reason, I felt compelled to use it for the mission aboard the *Abenteuer*. Maybe something inside me knew that I would be meeting you."

We both stare into each other's eyes for what seems like an eternity. Then Bob grunts, and we both look over at her.

"This is worse than a soap opera," she says. "Would you just kiss her already and put us all out of our misery?"

* * *

As Erich and I are coming up for air, an agent pokes

her head into the office. "Aunt C would like to speak with the two of you, sir," she says. "And we're ready to take the prisoner into custody."

The agent sets a metal case on the desk. She unlocks it and a screen pops up. She points at a large red button. "The secure line is activated. Press that to speak with headquarters."

After she wrestles Bob to her feet and ushers her out of the office, Erich initiates the call.

"Congratulations," Aunt C says to us. "Thanks to your efforts, the mission was a success. You captured the head of the Noveau Rougue Order, and we have stopped the terrorists from getting their hands on the weapons."

She pauses to listen to someone out of view. Turning back to us, she says, "Someone else wants to join the call."

I grin when I see General Taylor sit next to Aunt C. She doesn't look pleased to be crowded out.

"I understand you've been a busy lady, Isabelle," the general says. "You've done an exceptional job. The reports I've received have been glowing. I'd like you to consider coming back to work in intelligence for me."

Aunt C leans across the general so that her face fills the screen. "Don't answer until you hear our offer?"

I furrow my brow. "Your offer?"

The general tries to maneuver his face back into

the picture, but Aunt C is too nimble for him. "Isabelle," he says in a muffled voice. "Ours is the better offer."

Erich and I exchange glances while the two of them bicker.

"What do you want to do? It looks like you have options," he says to me. "Of course, there's always the mini-mart."

I elbow him in the ribs. "Do not ever mention the mini-mart again."

He holds up his hands. "I promise. So then which option are you going to choose—Air Force intelligence or a career with the organization?"

"It's an easy decision," I say. "The organization."

"Is that because you want to work with me?" Erich asks with a cocky grin on his face.

"Well, there's that," I say. "But I also heard you have a great dental plan."

Erich laughs, then points at Aunt C and the general continuing to argue about who I should work with. "Do you think they'd notice if we disconnected?"

"Not at all," I say, pressing the red button.

Erich closes the case, then pulls me into his arms. "Now about that dental plan . . ."

But before he can go into the details of whether root canals are covered, I silence him with a kiss.

EPILOGUE – ERICH
(SIX MONTHS LATER AT AN
UNDISCLOSED LOCATION)

Isabelle is sitting at the kitchen counter looking at her laptop when I sneak up behind her. But before I can put my hands over her eyes, she launches herself off her stool, does a back flip, and then executes a martial arts move I've never seen before. The end result is that I'm lying on the floor. I'd move, but Isabelle is pinning me down.

"Someone's been training," I say.

Isabelle snorts. "Someone's been slacking off on his training."

"I'm on vacation," I say. "It's the first one I've had in a very long time. Can't a fellow relax a little?"

"Just don't go getting soft on me," she jokes.

I give her a stupid grin. It's an expression that seems to make a regular appearance on my face ever since Isabelle came into my life. Isabelle grins back, her dark eyes sparkling. Not only is this woman beautiful, she's also whip-smart and every bit my equal when it comes to working in covert intelligence.

Okay, let's be real, here. She's a million times better than me in the spy game. Something Aunt C doesn't hesitate to remind me of on a regular basis. I'm lucky she's my partner at work, not to mention my partner in everything else outside of work.

"Ready to say uncle?" Isabelle asks.

"Yes, but on one condition," I say.

Isabelle arches an eyebrow. "What's the condition?"

"That you give me a kiss."

"Hmm, isn't a kiss you give someone as a reward?" Isabelle asks. "I'm not sure you should be rewarded for slacking off on your training."

"Oh, no, it wouldn't be a reward. It'd be a punishment. You're an awful kisser."

When Isabelle bursts out laughing, I take advantage of her loss of focus. Using one of my tried-and-true moves, I free my hands from her grasp, then reverse our position so that she's now lying on her back. I lower my face so that my lips are brushing against hers. "Now, about that kiss."

The timer on the oven buzzes, interrupting us. "Dinner's ready," I say, getting to my feet, then helping Isabelle to hers.

Isabelle sits back on her stool. "What are we

having?"

"Your favorite—baked potatoes," I say, peeking inside the oven. "I also made some schnitzel and there's strudel for dessert."

"Yum," Isabelle says as she pulls her laptop toward her.

"Your turn to cook tomorrow," I say.

"I have something special planned," Isabelle says. "Fondue. My friend in Switzerland sent me her recipe."

"Sounds good." I pull the potatoes out of the oven, then say, "It will be the last meal of our vacation. I heard from Aunt C. She has a new assignment for us. We're headed to South America. A terrorist group is threatening to sabotage a major cacao processing facility."

"That sounds serious," Isabelle says. "Interrupt the chocolate supply and you'll cause global chaos."

"That's why they're sending in the A-team." I set the plates on the counter. "Put your computer away, it's time to eat."

"Just a sec. I got an email from Sophia. She and Auguste Renoir set a wedding date." Isabelle looks up at me. "Thanks again for pulling strings so that Head Office made an exception and let them work on the riverboat together."

"It seemed like the right thing to do," I say. "After all, she covered for you the night of the mission in Basel."

While Isabelle replies to Sophia, I pour two glasses of riesling. As I take a sip, I reminisce about the first time Isabelle and I had riesling together. What a difference six months has made in her confidence. After the string of successful missions we've carried out over that period of time, I think Isabelle has realized what an asset she is to the organization. She believes in herself again.

After dinner, we do the dishes, then I tell Isabelle that I have a surprise for her in the other room "Go look at the coffee table."

As she walks through the archway that separates the kitchen from the living room, she laughs. "Is that a Scrabble board? But I thought you hated playing Scrabble."

"For you, I'll make an exception," I say, pulling her into my arms. After giving her a quick kiss, I motion for her to sit on the sofa. "Now, I can't exactly play at a championship level like you, so you'll have to be patient with me."

"First, we draw to see who goes first." Isabelle starts to grab for the bag of tiles, but I snatch it away from her.

"I'd like to go first, if you don't mind."

As I pull tiles out of the bag and arrange them on the board, Isabelle shakes her head. "That's not how you do it. We each draw seven tiles from the bag and place them on our racks."

"That's seven tiles." I spin the board around so

that she can see it. "Go ahead, count them."

"No, you have to put them . . ." her voice trails off as she looks down at what I've spelled out.

"What's my score?" I ask as I point at each tile in turn. "Let's see, there's M, A, R, R, Y, M, and E. Don't I get double or triple points for that?"

"Does that mean what I think it means?" Isabelle asks in a shaky voice.

"It means I want you to be my wife." I hand her the tile bag. "There's something else in there."

As she pulls the velvet jewelry box out, I hold my breath. What if she says no? Why would a woman as amazing as Isabelle want to spend the rest of her life with me?

She opens the box and pulls out the ring. After a beat, she asks, "Are those amethysts on either side of the diamond?"

"I know how much you love the amethyst ring your grandmother left you. I thought it would be nice if they coordinated." I take a deep breath. "You still haven't given me an answer. Will you marry me?"

Isabelle sets the engagement ring down on the board, then fishes through the bag of tiles. After a moment, she lays three letters down on the board—Y, E, and S. Then she slips the ring on her finger.

"You know, for a novice Scrabble player, you're actually pretty good at the game," she says, coming over and sitting on my lap. "Now, since you seem to have won that game, how about a reward?"

"Or is that a punishment?" I murmur in her ear before proceeding to kiss my new fiancée.

AUTHOR'S NOTE

Thank you so much for reading my book! If you enjoyed it, I'd be grateful if you would consider leaving a short review on the site where you purchased it and/or on Goodreads. Reviews help other readers find my books while also encouraging me to keep writing.

The *Smitten with Travel* romantic comedy series is inspired by my experiences living as an ex-pat for many years in Scotland and New Zealand and my travels, including my own "happily ever after" when my now-husband and I eloped to Denmark, followed by our honeymoon in Paris.

Many years ago, my husband and I went on a week-long cycling trip along the Rhine River. While I was struggling to pedal my bike, I would see the riverboats going up and down the river. It seemed like such a wonderful way to explore the amazing sites in this magnificent part of Europe. I've always dreamed of going back to the region and taking a riverboat cruise. Maybe one day, I'll make it happen, but in the meantime, I enjoyed living vicariously through Isabelle on her fictitious riverboat as she visited the various ports of call.

I want to thank my husband, Scott Jacobson, for his continued support and encouragement. He's the first person to read my manuscripts and his suggestions and ideas always make my books better. Many thanks as well to my editor, Beth Balmanno, for her keen eye and thoughtful edits.

And, of course, I couldn't do this without you—my wonderful readers. Your support and encouragement mean everything. I love to hear from readers, so please feel free to drop me an email at ellenjacobsonauthor@gmail.com.

ABOUT THE AUTHOR

Ellen Jacobson is a chocolate obsessed cat lover who writes cozy mysteries and romantic comedies. After working in Scotland and New Zealand for several years, she returned to the States, lived aboard a sailboat, traveled around in a tiny camper, and is now settled in a small town in northern Oregon with her husband and an imaginary cat named Simon.

Find out more at ellenjacobsonauthor.com

ALSO BY ELLEN JACOBSON

The Smitten with Travel Romantic Comedy Series

Smitten with Ravioli
Smitten with Croissants
Smitten with Strudel
Smitten with Candy Canes (Christmas Novella)

The Mollie McGhie Cozy Mystery Series

Robbery at the Roller Derby (Prequel Novella)
Murder at the Marina
Bodies in the Boatyard
Poisoned by the Pie
Buried by the Beach (Short Story)
Dead in the Dinghy
Shooting by the Sea
Overboard on the Ocean
Murder Aboard the Mistletoe (Christmas Novella)

The Mollie McGhie Cozy Mystery Collection: Books 1-3
The Mollie McGhie Cozy Mystery Collection: Books 4-6

Made in the USA
Coppell, TX
04 August 2022

80907811R00142